TRAVELERS
BY NIGHT

Also by Vivien Alcock

THE HAUNTING OF CASSIE PALMER
THE STONEWALKERS
THE SYLVIA GAME

TRAVELERS BY NIGHT

Vivien Alcock

DELACORTE PRESS / NEW YORK

Published by
Delacorte Press
1 Dag Hammarskjold Plaza
New York, N.Y. 10017

This work was first published in Great Britain by Methuen Children's Books Ltd.

MANUFACTURED IN THE UNITED STATES OF AMERICA
FIRST U.S.A. PRINTING

Library of Congress Cataloging in Publication Data
Alcock, Vivien.
    Travelers by night.
    Summary: Determined to save an old elephant from the slaughterhouse, two circus children kidnap the animal and begin a dangerous journey, traveling by night across the English countryside to a safari park where they hope to find the elephant a home.
    1. Children's stories, English. [1. Circus—Fiction. 2. Elephants—Fiction. 3. England—Fiction] I. Title.
PZ7.A334Tr   1985   [Fic]
ISBN 0-385-29406-9
Library of Congress Catalog Card Number: 85-1663

To Maggie and Peter

1

Although the early mist had gone and the sun was shining, the long grass at the side of the road was still wet. The ballerina, sparkling like a dragonfly in her spangled dress, peered down at it suspiciously, as if wondering what sharp stones and rusty tins might be lurking beneath the foxgloves.

"Best not sit down," she said.

"Don't fuss." The clown parted the grass with his foot, kicked an old Coke tin into the hedge, and sniffed. "No thistles," he said.

"Grass stains won't come out easy," she said sharply. "You stay on your feet. And pull your trousers up, they're soaked at the bottom. I'll have the skin off you if you get all mucked up."

"Don't fuss," he said again, but bent down obediently to pull his baggy, frilled trousers up to his knees, revealing bare brown legs, smudged with dirt.

"You never washed!" she said accusingly.

"I did. First thing." He looked at his legs reflectively. "Dunno where that comes from."

"Been fighting again, I bet."

"What, me? Never!" the boy said, turning a mock innocent face toward her. Although he was dressed in the traditional costume of a true clown, with a wide, white ruff around his neck and a conical hat on top of his bushy hair, he wore no greasepaint. A white papier-mâché mask was pushed up on his forehead like a visor, above a thin, freckled face that shone as if it had been scrubbed with cold water and the soap not all rinsed away. "Don't nag at me, Belle. Who are we doing this for, anyway?"

"Me."

"Just you remember that. I said I'd see you right, didn't I?"

"Yes, Charlie."

Her voice was flat. He glanced at her sharply, but she was already wearing her golden mask and her face was as blank as an idol's.

"I *will*, you know," he said. "Swear to God . . ."

Suddenly he was depressed, seeing his promise stretch like a shadow over the uncertain years ahead. Every penny they earned went into their secret fund, but the sum they needed was enormous. If only he were grown-up and could work full-time. Soon, indeed, they wouldn't be able to work at all. At the end of the week, their world was coming to an end. Peachem's Circus was folding. It had gone bust, unable even to stagger on until the end of the season. A

wet July, too many debts, and no one willing to give
credit . . .

Moodily he kicked a pebble into the roadside opposite. It was a good site he had chosen; a long stretch
of road, a roadside opposite for their act. The only
trouble was, the service lane was empty, the road was
empty, the whole damn world was empty, except for
a couple of birds in the sky, and *they* had no money.

"Where are they?" he said. "What's happened to
everyone around here?"

"Dunno," Belle said. "Unless it's the Bomb. Perhaps they're all blown up and we're the only ones left.
You and me, Charlie." She had picked a white morning glory out of the hedge, and was twisting it around
and around in her fingers. "Only we won't last long.
It's all contaminated, see?" She held the flower out
toward his cheek. "One touch and you'll burn!"

"Oh, shut up!" he said impatiently. He hated the
way she talked about death, with sly relish, as if it
fascinated her. She did it on purpose, of course. He
wasn't stupid. He knew she was getting at him. She
might as well have said out loud, You saved my life.
Don't think you've done me a favor. I'd just as soon
be dead.

"I wish . . ." he began furiously, when she interrupted him, looking toward the corner.

"Car coming."

He could hear it now.

"Ready, Belle?"

"Yes."

He pulled the white mask down over his face, and they stood poised, waiting.

Mr. Barker was driving up the hill toward the corner.

"Well, it's nice to see the sun again, isn't it?" said his wife.

"Yes."

They were on holiday, the same family holiday they had every year, in one little seaside town or another. They were all alike, these holidays; the same six days of rain, the same one fine day . . .

"Can we have a picnic on the beach, Daddy?"

Why not? he thought. We always do. Even in a point nine gale.

"That sounds splendid," he said aloud.

The same gravelly sand, the same cold gray sea. The same gritty sandwiches, the annual tragedy of the dropped ice cream . . .

"Don't you sometimes wish," he said to his wife, "that you could turn a corner and see something utterly different?"

"How do you mean, dear?"

"Oh, I don't know." He changed down into third gear for the sharp bend at the top of the hill. Surprise me, Fate, he thought.

Now there was a long, straight stretch of road, running between tangled hedges, the grass verges full of foxgloves, buttercups, and purple vetch.

"Look! Oh, Daddy, look!"

Some way ahead, two glittering figures had stepped

out into the road. One bowed and one curtsied. Then they cartwheeled neatly into an empty service lane and began to dance.

"What are they, Daddy? What are they doing?"

They were like hummingbirds in their brilliant sequined costumes, wheeling and dipping and somersaulting beneath the blue parking sign. Mr. Barker drove slowly toward them, staring. One of them, a clown, was now running backward, beckoning with his arms, inviting them into the roadside, while the ballerina danced on alone in her golden mask.

"He wants us to stop, Daddy! Please, Daddy! Can we, Daddy?"

The car drew into the roadside, and the doors opened. Behind the clown's white mask two shrewd eyes assessed the family as they got out. Two little girls, flushed and excited, a boy of about ten, fancying himself too old for enjoyment. The mother—not so good! Spends all her money on her back and wants value for it. The father—hey, here's a fine, smiling gentleman for you! Good for a pound at the very least. A fiver, if we're lucky.

The clown and the ballerina joined hands, bowed, and began their act. Mr. Barker watched them in pleased astonishment.

"They must be from the circus." his wife said, "There were posters up in the last village, did you notice? I suppose they'll want money."

Of course, she was right, thought Mr. Barker, they must be circus children. They were not, after all, shining visitors from a brighter world. The boy's legs were dirty, and the girl's barrette was made of pink plastic. Still, they were charming, dancing in the sunlight in their flamboyant costumes. They might have stepped out of any century, wayside acrobats amazing travelers with their tinseled skills. When he was a boy, he had once dreamed of running off to join a circus.

"They're good." he said.

Their act was simple enough. The clown was in love with the ballerina. He pressed his hands to his heart, blew her kisses, walked upside down, and somersaulted before her but all in vain. She did not seem to see him but danced as if in a dream, serious and self-absorbed.

"Why won't she look at him, Daddy?"

"I don't know, dear."

Now the clown held his hand in the air, shook it, and a red rose blossomed in his fingers. He offered it to the ballerina. Still ignoring him, she did a high kick, and the flower shot from his hand. As he bent to pick it up another dancing kick sent him staggering forward. He straightened up, rubbing his behind, and a third kick narrowly missed knocking off his hat. The children laughed.

Cold water and hard knocks for the clowns, Punch beating Judy . . . there was always cruelty.

The ballerina had danced away, leaving the clown disconsolate, holding the rejected flower in his hand. He turned his back on the dancer and, coming forward, offered the paper rose to the smallest girl. Perhaps it was the white mask that frightened her. She shrank away from him and hid her face in her mother's skirts.

"She's shy," Mrs. Barker said. "Don't you want the pretty flower, Jenny? I'll take it for you, shall I?"

The little girl peeped and nodded.

"I want one, too." It was the second little girl, her face about ready to cry. At any moment she'd wail that it wasn't fair.

Life isn't fair, Charlie could have told her. And these flowers don't grow on bushes, you know. Your daddy'd better pay well.

He brought his hand out from behind his back, flicked his fingers, and there was another rose, blue this time. Now the older boy had come up—don't say *he* wanted a flower! No, he only wanted to tell Charlie how the trick worked.

"You've got them in your back pocket," he said. "They're folded flat and you sort of shake them out. I saw! It's not much of a trick."

Clever little snot! Let him try it with sweating fingers and the thin paper all too ready to stick and tear.

"It was splendid," Mr. Barker said. "I enjoyed it." He put his hand in his pocket. Charlie held out his hat hopefully. Now Belle came dancing up beside him, all gold and yellow and shining. She sank into a deep curtsy.

The smallest girl, fascinated, toddled up to her on fat legs. "Pretty," she said, and put out her hand to touch the golden mask. Belle jerked her head away sharply, but the child's fingers had caught in the elastic and it snapped. The mask fell off.

The child stared, her face crumpling. Then she burst into tears and ran back to her mother.

"What's that on her face?" whispered the other girl, too audibly.

"It's a scar, silly," said the boy. "What did you think it was? A worm?"

The clown sprang on him, and, knocking him to the ground, began punching his head.

2

Her son was yelling for help, but Mrs. Barker could not move. Her two small daughters, crying and clinging to her, kept her anchored to the ground.

"Do something, Bill!" she shouted to her husband, who just stood there like a dolt while their son was being punched to pieces. "Do something!"

Mr. Barker caught hold of Charlie's arm and pulled him roughly to his feet. There was the sound of ripping cloth. Immediately Mr. Barker's back was pummeled by hard, furious fists. The ballerina was attacking him, shouting:

"You're tearing it! You're tearing it! He's got to wear it tonight!"

Looking around, he thought for a startled moment that her head was on back to front. But then, seeing the tip of her nose just visible, he realized that she had hidden her scarred face behind curtains of hair. Oh, poor girl! he thought with a pang. Then he felt a sharper pain as Charlie bit his hand. He yelped and let go of the boy's arm.

"Run!" shouted Charlie, and fled.

Let them try to catch us, he thought, knowing he was fast. When he reached the gap in the hedge on the other side of the road and looked back, he saw the family had hardly moved. But Belle—Belle, who should have been at his heels, being as fast as he was, was now lying on the ground. Blinded by her own hair, she had tripped and fallen.

"Come on!" he shouted.

In answer she made a furious gesture that said as plainly as words, Get out of sight. He hesitated, then obediently pushed through the gap in the hedge and, crouching down opposite the roadside, looked through the leaves.

Belle seemed in no hurry. She had picked herself up and was now examining her leg. Charlie saw her wipe away a trickle of blood before it reached her yellow satin pump. Blood, like grass stains, did not wash out easily. Then she turned to look at the man.

"He bit me!" Mr. Barker was saying, sounding astonished. "Look, it's bleeding."

Belle took his hand in her dusty fingers and peered at it through her hair.

"That's nothing. Scarce broke the skin," she said, unable to keep the scorn from her voice. "You won't die. He cleaned his teeth this morning."

"I'm glad to hear it," Mr. Barker said.

The little girls had been bundled into the back of

the car, their wailing now muffled with chocolate. Mrs. Barker was holding a handkerchief to her son's bloody nose.

"Come and sit down, Donald," she said. "Tilt your head back. I'll guide you to the car."

"Best throw cold water over him," advised Belle. It was difficult to tell whether she was suggesting a cure or a drowning. Mrs. Barker turned on her furiously.

"You're from that circus, aren't you? I've a good mind to complain. I wonder what they'll say when they hear how you've behaved. . . ."

"*Me?*" Belle said. "I done nothing! I'm the injured party. I've been insulted, I have!"

"My dear, I'm sure Donald never meant . . ." Mr. Barker began.

"He said I got a worm on my face!"

"I didn't! I said it wasn't a worm!"

"You got no call to mention worms at all!" shouted Belle, her voice thick with tears.

"I didn't mean . . ." the boy began, but his mother pulled him toward the car, telling him not to argue with that girl, he was only making matters worse, getting blood all over his shirt.

Mr. Barker looked at Belle. Her lowered head was moving slowly from side to side, her face completely covered by her hair. He thought that she was weeping behind it and wished desperately that he could comfort her. Had she been his daughter, he could have put his arms around her and told her it didn't matter, everything would be all right. But he could think of nothing to say to this sad circus child.

"There it is!" She bent down suddenly and picked up a pink plastic barrette from the ground, with which she then fastened back her hair from the un-damaged side of her face. He could see the tear tracks still damp on her cheek, but her one visible eye was now dry.

"Did Charlie take his hat?" she asked.

"I don't know. I'm afraid I didn't notice. It doesn't seem to be here."

"Must've done, then. Was there anything in it?"

"What?" He looked at her blankly.

"*Money!* Did you pay him, mister?"

"Oh! No, I was just going to when—"

"You owe us, mister," she said. "You saw the show. You tore Charlie's costume. And you're standing on my mask."

He looked down guiltily and saw that the golden mask was under his toe. "Sorry." He picked it up and handed it to her, then said with awkward pity, "You don't need a mask, my dear. You're a very pretty girl—"

"Sure. Like the fairy on top of the Christmas tree—after the cat's got it." Her voice was hard. He saw that she did not want his sympathy, only his money, and got out his wallet. She watched his fingers hover over the one-pound notes.

"It's for my face," she confided, sounding suddenly different, her voice now soft, pathetically childish. "That's what we're doing this for, see? We're saving up so's I can have it fixed up proper. In Harley Street, where all the nobs go. Charlie says I'm to have the best," she added proudly. Seeing that his fingers had moved on to the fives, she said, letting her voice tremble, "Only it costs such a lot." His fingers stopped.

"Don't!" he said sharply. "Please don't!"

She looked puzzled. "Don't what, mister?"

"Don't . . . oh, it doesn't matter." How could he tell her not to beg for pity, using her scar like a leper displaying his sores or a freak in a sideshow? She was, after all, a circus child, trained to perform. Turning his back so that his wife could not see what he was doing, he extracted two fives from his wallet and dropped them into the waiting hand.

"What are you doing, Bill?" came his wife's suspicious voice from the car.

"Nothing, dear," Mr. Barker said, and saw the circus child smile.

"Thanks. Thanks a lot," she whispered, and then urgently, "You won't let her tell on us, will you? Only they'd be wild if they knew what we'd been up to. It's a secret, see? You don't want to get us into trouble, do you, mister?"

"No," he said, "don't worry."

"Thanks."

He watched her run lightly across the road and vanish through the hedge.

"Bill!" his wife called. "Bill!"

"Coming, dear," he said.

Charlie had already changed when Belle came through the hedge and was examining his costume ruefully.

"Let's see," she said, "is it torn bad?"

He showed it to her, putting his fingers through the long slit.

"Can you mend it for me, Belle?" he asked anxiously. His own large, staggering stitches would never escape notice. She nodded.

"Easy. It's only the seam that's gone," she said. "You'll have to wash it, though. It's filthy. What did you want to go rolling around in the dirt for? After I'd warned you, too."

He had done it for her but knew better than to say so. He had seen the look on her face before she had hidden it with her long hair, and just had to punch someone. Anyone. He had tried to count up to ten, as he'd promised the boss he would, after his last fight, but it was no use. His fists would not wait for his slow arithmetic: he had gotten no further than three before he had knocked the boy down.

"I'm not sorry," he said stubbornly.

She turned her back on him and began taking off her yellow sequined dress. She had lost weight since the accident, and her backbone showed up like a string of ivory beads.

Charlie folded up his dusty costume and put it in the bottom of his bucket. It was Belle who had suggested using buckets. "Walk off empty-handed and they'll catch us for some chore or other," she had said. "But if we carry buckets, they'll think someone else got us first. We can smuggle out our fancies easy."

"Suppose they look inside?" he had asked, worried

at the idea of using their best costumes for their private performances, knowing it would double their crime in the boss's eyes.

But Belle had only laughed. "We'll put lids on the buckets and screw up our noses like they stink," she had said. "That'll keep them off."

It had. So far they had been lucky.

He looked back at Belle. She was fastening the buttons of her blue dress, her yellow costume lying in the grass at her feet like an enormous buttercup. He picked it up and began folding it.

"Leave that. I'll do it," she said. "Look in your hat, Charlie."

He had left his hat, perched upside down on a clump of meadowsweet. When he reached for it, he saw the money she had put inside.

"Ten pounds! *Ten pounds!*" he said, astonished. "I never expected . . . I thought I'd blown it!"

She said nothing.

"Belle, you're a marvel. Clever Belle," he said admiringly, wanting to please her. "How on earth did you wangle it?"

"He was a soft touch," she said, then burst into tears.

He did not know what to do. Belle never cried. Never! Not after the accident, with the blood streaming down her cheek. Not in the hospital, with her face all wrapped in bandages, looking like the invisible man. Not once since he had first met her . . .

He had been five years old then. He remembered standing, peeping through the tent door into the strange big top, bewildered, frightened, and miserable. His parents had been killed in a road accident, and now his Uncle Bert and his Auntie Annie were going to look after him.

"You'll soon feel at home here, dear," they had said, trying to comfort him. "It's not as if you're leaving circus life. We're all one big family, aren't we? And there's our Belle—she'll be a sister for you. You'll like that, won't you?"

He had nodded and sniffed, but he had not wanted a sister. He had wanted his mother and father back, and their own circus; not this small shabby one where they didn't even have big cats, only three elephants and a chimpanzee. He had peered sulkily through the tent door.

"There she is. On the Shetland," they had said.

She was dressed in a froth of silver lace and had scarlet flowers in her golden hair. He thought he had never seen anything so beautiful. Not that she had done very much, being as young as he was. She had ridden once around the ring, kneeling on the back of her pony, and then had risen, very shakily, to her feet, with the catcher running beside her, looking anxious until she sat down again with a bump. But the audience had loved her and cheered her as she came riding out of the ring.

Her face was flushed with the pleasure of her success. She had jumped down from her pony and handed the ribbons to a ringman with all the assurance of a young princess. Then she had caught sight of Charlie and stopped. For a moment she had stared

at him curiously while he gazed back at her, speechless. Then she had smiled and come running toward
him, her hands outstretched.

"You're Charlie, ain't you?" she had said. "You're
my new brother." And she had kissed him. But even
then he had not wanted her for a sister.

"I'm going to marry you when I grow up," he had
told her, and everyone had laughed, while Belle had
tossed her head and said, "You'll be lucky." But he
had known she was pleased.

He looked at her now, all these years later, a thin
girl in a faded dress, weeping over her discarded
finery, and his heart ached.

"Oh, stow it, Belle," he said awkwardly. "Stop
sniveling. It isn't the end of the world."

"It is!" she said through her tears. "I don't want to
leave. I don't want to go to no new school where
they'll all stare at me. I want to stay with the circus."

"We'll think of something," he said, but he knew it
was no good. They would have to go.

3

There was no matinee that afternoon. Peachem's Circus was dozing in the sun. The artistes sat outside their trailers, their aproned laps filled with finery that needed a stitch, or props wanting a screw tightened or a leather strap adjusted. In the box office Mrs. Clarke yawned, frowned at the pile of unsold tickets, and then glanced, without much hope, at a group of children hanging around outside the entrance.

"Still a few seats left," she called encouragingly. "Book now to make sure of getting in."

They smiled and shuffled their feet.

"Can we go and have a look at the animals?" one of them asked.

"Sorry, dear. Not this afternoon."

Belle and Charlie came into sight. Belle was limping slightly. Charlie carried his bucket as though it were very heavy. They looked, quite convincingly, as if they had been running errands all afternoon and it would be unkind to expect them to do another thing.

"Excuse us. Mind your legs. Make way, please," they said.

The loitering children turned to look at them.

"Do you work here?" a small boy asked, a look of wistful envy in his round eyes.

"Yes," Belle said proudly, "Cosmo and Christobel, the Star Spinners, that's us."

"Go on!"

"It's true. Come and see us tonight. I might blow you a kiss."

She seemed in high spirits. There was no trace of tears left on her uncovered cheek. But as always, her hair concealed the left side of her face, hanging close to her nose like half a golden mask. Charlie sometimes wondered whether, if he pushed it back, he would find the hidden eye weeping for her lost beauty, even while she smiled.

"What's in them buckets?" another boy asked.

"Champagne for the elephants."

"Carry it for you, miss?" he offered hopefully. Belle laughed and shook her head.

As they passed the box office Mrs. Clarke looked at them benevolently.

"Still hard at work, I see," she said.

"Just about finished," said Charlie.

"That's good. Do with a rest, I expect."

They smiled and hurried on. But they were not safe yet. The fine day had brought too many people out.

Three grooms, lying in the grass outside the stable tent, watched them pass.

"Hey, is that water?" said one, getting to his feet. "Come on, hand it over."

"Fetch your own," Charlie said, fending him off as the man reached for the bucket.

For water was in great demand. Their agent, perhaps because he had not been paid for some time, had had it installed, not in the field itself, but halfway up the lane.

"It ain't water, anyhow. It's dirty washing," Belle said. "And you can have it over your head with pleasure."

"Little spitfire," the groom said, laughing.

They hurried on, wishing they were invisible. They had nearly reached the property wagons when Belle's mother stepped out from behind a trailer.

"There you are," she said. "I've been looking for you everywhere."

She was a plump, pretty woman, with rosy cheeks and bleached yellow hair, now hidden by a striped towel. She looked hot and rather cross. Then she noticed the buckets in their hands, and her eyes brightened. "Water! Bless you, my loves, just what—"

"Sorry, Mum," Belle said hastily, holding her bucket out of her mother's reach. "It's promised. It's for . . ." The warm, musky, familiar smell of elephants came from the tent beside her. "It's for the elephants. Mr. Murphy sent us for it."

"Your mother comes first. He can make do with one bucket."

"It ain't water, it's—it's apples."

"Vegetable scraps," said Charlie at the same time.

Mrs. Marriot looked from one to the other suspiciously.

"We'll get you some water later. Promise," Belle said, and pulled Charlie into the tent, knowing that her mother would not follow. Unlike Belle, Mrs. Marriot was not overly fond of elephants. It was no good everyone telling her they walked on their huge, baggy legs as daintily as cats. The sight of a foot, big as a barrel, coming down anywhere near her painted toenails made her, she said, feel ill.

After the bright sunlight, it was dark inside the tent. They could see dimly the huge gray bulk of the three elephants and the white patches on the Shetland pony from whom one of them, Stella, refused to be parted.

"No one here," Belle said. "That's a bit of luck. We can hide till she's gone."

There was a rustling in the straw as the three great creatures shifted their feet. The largest, recognizing Belle, stretched out her trunk in greeting. This was Tessie, an old animal with a ragged ear and a loving heart, whom Belle had known as long as she could remember. She often came to her, when she was in trouble, taking comfort from the enormous, gentle creature. As she walked up to her now, searching her pocket for a titbit, a voice said, "And who are you hiding from?"

Two men stepped out of the shadows and came toward them. One was Mr. Murphy, the animal trainer. He wasn't so bad. Though it was well known that he liked elephants first, snakes second, and boys not at all, he had a soft spot for Belle. The man who had spoken was another matter. Hugo Schneider was the star of the show, considered by some to be the finest tightrope walker in the world. It was said that he had only come to Peachem's because he was an old friend of the boss's and already had a fine new job waiting. He was also the children's trainer, a stern, tall man, with sleek fair hair and eyes as sharp as pins.

"Well?" he said.

"We d-didn't see you," Belle stammered.

"That is obvious. You haven't answered my question."

But Mr. Murphy had noticed their buckets.

"Water," he said gratefully. "Now that was a kind thought."

"We'll fetch you some water, Mr. Murphy. Right away, Mr. Murphy," they said, edging toward the tent door.

Mr. Schneider stretched out a long arm and blocked their way.

"You know, Danny, I think those buckets are empty," he said to the animal trainer. Mr. Murphy nodded.

"The bucket dodge," he said.

"I have suspected it for a long time," Mr. Schneider said. "I have never seen two children so attached to buckets. They carry them everywhere. I don't know who they think they are fooling."

The animal trainer shook his head sadly.

"Shirkers, that's what they are. Never would've thought it of them. Little Belle, now, always helping me with my fat friends. Shame on you, girl. Carrying around empty buckets, pretending to work and all the time sneaking off the site."

Belle hung her head. Don't let them ask to look in them, she prayed, glad that the lids were tightly on. Don't let them find our costumes!

Then, to her astonishment, she heard the men laugh.

"Lord, we were on the bucket dodge long before you were born," Mr. Schneider said. "Weren't we, Danny?"

The animal trainer nodded. "Oldest trick in the world. Things don't change much. Or only for the worse," he added, half under his breath, looking suddenly as gray and wrinkled as one of his beloved elephants. "I never thought to see the end of Peachem's Circus. Thought it would last out our time, didn't we, Tessie, old girl?" The elephant reached out with her trunk and nuzzled him gently.

"I'll do what I can, Danny," said Mr. Schneider. "But . . ."

"I know. I know. These are bad times, Hugo. Not to worry. I hear your Mom and Dad are fixed up in America, Belle?" he said.

The children, thinking themselves forgotten, had been edging toward the tent door. They stopped.

"Well, sort of," Belle said. "Uncle Bob said he'd try

and find them something in his show, but . . . it'll just be helping around at first. Not a proper billing."

"Lucky to find anything these days," said the old man. "Are you going with them?"

Belle shook her head.

"Auntie Annie says they'll have to see how it works out," Charlie explained. "We're to stay with our Auntie May and go to school regular."

"I don't know what for," Belle muttered. "I can read and write and do sums. But Dad says we got to be educated proper."

Mr. Schneider smiled at the bitterness in her voice. "A terrible fate. You have my sympathy," he said. "Off with you now. Practice tomorrow. It'll be the last one, so see that you're there. *Both* of you."

Belle looked guilty. She had often skipped practice since her accident and thought no one had noticed.

"Yes, you, too, Belle. I have something I want to say to you all."

"Wonder what?" she said when she and Charlie had left the tent.

"Probably wants to say good-bye."

"Good-bye," she repeated, and shivered in the bright sunlight. She looked around at the circle of trailers and trucks and painted wagons, at the big top with its brave blue-and-white stripes, its yellow flags stirring idly in the soft wind. She could not believe it was all coming to an end.

4

The next morning was wet and windy again. Belle, sitting by herself in a ringside seat, could hear the rain beating on the canvas above her head, while all around her the big top shook, straining at its moorings as if impatient to be gone. She wished it would sail away, taking her with it. She was cold and bored.

In the ring, the Cosmic Kids were going through their routine on the trampoline, looking like Mexican jumping beans. She had been a Cosmic Kid once. Now, thank the Lord, she was too old for it. Poor Charlie, promoted to catcher, was hanging upside down from the low trapeze, his freckled face already as red as a strawberry.

"No! No! No!" Mr. Schneider was saying to young Lily Reeves. "Your timing is all wrong. On the *backward* swing, how many times must I tell you? Try again. Don't look at me, look at Charlie! Now, one and two and three . . ." he counted as the little girl began her jumps, "and *up!*" He banged his hands down on the trampoline, and Lily shot up in the air. Charlie caught her neatly, swung her backward and then forward into a high somersault. She muffed it, twisting awkwardly in midair, coming down too near the edge of the trampoline and bouncing off sideways. Mr. Schneider caught her before she hit the sawdust, spun her around like a pinwheel, and set her on her feet.

"Smile!" he commanded. "Hold your arms up to the audience as if you're clever, instead of a clumsy little dolt."

The audience, that's me, Belle thought, and I ain't going to clap. Bet she tries to blame it on Charlie . . . yes, there she goes.

"It wasn't my fault," Lily Reeves was saying in her high, whining voice. "Charlie threw me crooked."

"I didn't!" Charlie sat up on his trapeze indignantly. "You messed it up like you always do."

"I didn't!"

"Did!"

"That's enough," Mr. Schneider said, holding up his hand. "We will have no fighting, please. You are supposed to be artistes, not monkeys. All right, all of you. Get your jackets on and then come and sit here. I have something I want to say to you."

He's forgotten our act, Belle thought joyfully. She sat down quickly behind the other children, trying to make herself as small and unnoticeable as possible.

"Did you see that . . ." Charlie said, thumping down beside her, "the stupid little—"

"Shh!"

"I thought I would talk to you today," Mr. Schneider began, "because tomorrow we will have no time. Tomorrow we have a matinee, an evening show; and then, the final pull-down. We go our separate ways . . ."

Charlie was right; a good-bye speech, Belle thought, bored. Why doesn't he get on with it—no need to make a big performance. We've heard it all before. Good-bye and thank you. You've been a pleasure to work with . . . real little troopers . . . a grand bunch of kids, et cetera and so on. She yawned and looked into the ring.

Oh, no! Two ringmen were spreading the blue-and-crimson carpet over the sawdust. She tried to catch their attention so that she could signal to them to take it away, but they did not look at her. Now they were bringing on the seesaw and assembling the high ramp for the Star Spinners act. Take it back! Quick, before he sees, she thought, wishing she could throw the silent words into their thick heads.

"Some of you, most of you, perhaps," Mr. Schneider was saying, "must face the fact that you may never get another circus job."

Belle turned to stare at him. *What?* This was not part of the usual good-bye speech.

"These are difficult times," he went on. "Peachem's is not the only circus to close down. Three went bust last year. Others are struggling. There will be fewer jobs, fiercer competition. Think about it. Decide now what you want to do. There are other careers, better paid, less demanding. Think about it."

The children fidgeted and looked serious, trying to think as they had been directed but finding their minds distracted by more immediate concerns. Lily Reeves was putting her tongue out at Charlie. Tim Clarke wanted to spend a penny. Mary Roget was scratching her head, worried in case she had gotten lice. Belle tried to think of nothing, a big, round nothing that kept turning into a circus ring.

"Those of you who decide you do want to stay on in the circus will have to work. Work, work, and more work," Mr. Schneider said. "Most of you will be out for a time, but you can't afford to be idle. Practice. Practice at home, practice in gymnasiums . . ."

Just a pep talk, thought Belle, bored again, and looked away. The ringmen were now rolling in the two huge globes, blue and covered with yellow stars, like gigantic beachballs. Damn! Still, perhaps there would not be time, she thought, glancing at her watch. Madame Nanette and her Performing Poodles had booked the ring for eleven.

"That's all, children. You may go now," said Mr. Schneider. The children scrambled to their feet and crowded, chattering and laughing, toward the tent door. Belle had almost reached it when she heard Mr. Schneider call, "Not you, Charlie! Stay behind, please."

She turned around. Surely he was not going to tell Charlie off for that catch? Any fool could tell him it had been Lily Reeves's fault. *She* would be that fool, if necessary.

Mr. Schneider, catching sight of her, hesitated and then said, "Yes. All right. You, too, Belle."

They came up to him, a little nervously, wondering which of their various misdeeds had been found out. But though he looked serious, he did not seem to be angry.

"First you, Charlie," he said. "I'm quite pleased with you. I've been watching you. You've improved. In fact, you're not bad, not bad at all." Charlie flushed with astonishment and delight. Mr. Schneider went on, "It would be a pity for you to give up now. So what I wanted to say is . . . well, I expect you've heard that I'm going to join Mayer's when I leave here. Remember, I shall be a new boy. My word will not count for much at first. But for what it's worth, it's yours. If you are looking for a holiday job at Christmas, come and see me. Mind, I promise nothing. There may be nothing. But it's worth a try, yes?" Seeing Charlie was speechless with pleasure, he smiled and said, "Okay?"

Charlie stammered his thanks, beaming. Then he looked at Belle uncertainly, a little anxious now.

Belle was smiling, too, a smile of pure, unselfish joy in another's success. It felt as if it were fastened to her face with nails, which made it difficult to speak. But she must say something. She did not want to spoil his pleasure.

"Good old Charlie," she said, and listened to the sound of her own voice, bright, clear, no smudge of envy to be heard. Clap hands, everybody, she thought, that was my finest performance. She was rewarded when Charlie's smile widened again.

"Run along, now, Charlie," Mr. Schneider said, "and don't boast to the other children or they'll all be around my neck. Off with you! I want to speak to Belle alone."

Charlie ran out, in great, springing steps, as if he were about to fly. They watched him go in silence. Then Mr. Schneider sighed.

"Belle, I am sorry," he said slowly. "I have nothing good to say to you. When I first came here, I found you the young star, brilliant, born for the spotlight; everyone told me. Yes, you were good. You were also the vainest, most tiresome brat I'd ever met. But you had talent."

Belle stared sulkily at her feet.

"What has happened to you?" Mr. Schneider went on. "I watch you now and you are nothing. Even Lily Reeves is better. Oh, it is not your scar," he said, seeing her hand go up to the hair that concealed it. "Your scar has done you a favor. You are not so proud. What is a scar in the circus? Greasepaint, a few sequins stuck on, and it's gone. But courage, courage you need. We can't afford passengers in the ring." Belle hung her head and said nothing. "You've lost your nerve, Belle, haven't you?" he asked gently.

"No! No, I ain't! I just need time. . . ."

"Time? Too much time is bad. Fall down, get up again, that's the only way."

"How could I? I was in the hospital."

"And when you came out of the hospital, what then? Did you go up the ramp? No. You were too tired, you had a headache, your tummy was upset. Excuses, always excuses. I was too soft with you, I think. No, leave that, please!" he added in a sharp voice.

Belle looked up, startled, and saw that he was addressing the two ringmen, who had come back and were about to dismantle the ramp.

"It's five to eleven, Squire," said one of them.

"So we have five minutes."

"But Madame Nanette . . ."

"Must wait."

The ringmen shrugged and left.

Mr. Schneider turned back to Belle. "It's not the high wire we are talking about," he said. "You had no business on the high wire, you know that now. I blame myself. I should've seen that it was taken down. But this is only the ramp. You have done it a hundred times before. Look at it! It is not so high, is it? What happens if you fall? I catch you. Don't you trust me?"

"Yes," she said, sounding so doubtful that he shrugged and said, "All right, say I miss you. What then? A few bruises, at worst a broken bone. Is that so bad?"

"No."

"You say you need more time. There *is* no more time. Tomorrow we close. Now you must do it. Fasten back your hair. You must be able to see properly. Come on, I've seen your scar. I've seen worse scars than yours. That's better. Now, what's this?" he said as she still hung back. "You are afraid? You are a little coward?"

"No!" she said, and took his outstretched hand.

He steadied her as she jumped up onto one of the globes and set it moving with her feet. Then he let go and watched her as she circled the carpet, balancing easily on the spinning ball. She began to move toward the seesaw, but he stopped her, saying, "I know you can still do that, and we're short of time. The ramp, please."

She hesitated, the ball slowing beneath her feet.

"Now!" he shouted furiously.

She started up the first slope, looking down at her feet, seeing the yellow stars whirling beneath her bare toes, around and around. . . . It was the stars, the stars were making her giddy. She glanced up and found that she was reaching the first bend. Steady, steady! She let the ball slow, her feet fumbling as she changed direction, so that it hit the side of the ramp and nearly unbalanced her. Oh, please, please don't roll back! She thrust her legs down like pistons, forcing the ball forward and up. To think she'd once fooled around on the ramp, letting herself roll backward deliberately toward Charlie, coming up behind her. Stopping just before the globes collided, making the audience gasp. She'd *enjoyed* it then. Must've been mad!

How much farther? She glanced up. Saw the big top spinning as if someone had set a whip to it. Her ball hit the side again and wobbled beneath her feet. Oh, God, she was going to fall. . . . Where was Mr. Schneider? She looked down and saw him beneath her, his pale upturned face blurring in the whirling shadows. . . . There seemed to be several Mr. Schneiders now, dancing in a ring, around and around, and shouting in her ears. . . . Why were there so many Mr. Schneiders?

"Charlie, help me!" she cried, and fell.

Mr. Schneider caught her as she landed on him with a thud that knocked the breath out of her and must have hurt him because he grunted. But he swung her over in a somersault and set her on her feet.

"Smile!" he said. "Hold up your arms and smile!"

She smiled. She held her arms up to the rows of empty seats and smiled, and wanted to be sick.

"That's my girl," he said, ruffling her hair.

"I tried!" she said. "I did my best, honest."

"I know you did, Belle. You were very brave. You're a good girl," he said gently. But he did not ask her to come to him for a job at Christmas. He did not ask her to try the ramp again. He knew she was finished.

Belle pulled the band out of her hair, letting it fall over her face, and rushed blindly out through the tent door.

Mr. Schneider looked after her.

What have I done? he thought. There was a

chance. I thought it might work, but . . . Poor child, what damage have I done?

"Mr. Schneider," said Madame Nanette, coming into the ring with a flurry of yelping, leaping poodles. "Mr. Schneider, you have stayed too long."

5

The big top was down; only a discolored circle showed where it had been. The painted buses, trucks, and trailers had driven away in heavy rain, leaving in the gateway a weirdly patterned moonscape of mud. Slowly, as the weeks passed, the flattened grass recovered. Five cows now grazed where once the elephants had walked. Nothing was left of Peachem's World Famous Circus except a sodden paper rose, blooming improbably in a hedge. Belle and Charlie's world had ended.

Charlie was glad it was over. Since it had to end, he wished it could have ended more quickly; that he and Belle, after the last performance, could have been precipitated, like Cosmic Kids off the trampoline, into Aunt May's waiting hands. It was terrible having to go to their winter quarters, arriving so unseasonably in the summer rain. The farmer's wife, who usually welcomed them with warm smiles and hot supper, had seemed distinctly chilly. Perhaps she felt that failure was catching. Perhaps she was worried in case she would not get paid. The elephants especially, whom in the past she had professed to admire, now came in for cold glances, as if she were afraid Mr. Murphy would sneak off in the night, leaving her with three mountainous, unpaying guests.

"Whatever will you do with them?" she said. "I mean, if you can't get another job. Not that they're not welcome to stay here for a week or two, but you'll want to be making other arrangements."

Even when the weather changed and became bright and warm, she remained as cool and sharp as one of her own kitchen knives. "Mr. Murphy, about them elephants . . ." she said yet again.

"Don't you worry, Mrs. Thorpe," he said, trying to sound cheerful and not altogether succeeding. "Two of them have found good homes already. Going to a circus in Germany. They'll be off on Wednesday."

"You ain't selling them?" Belle burst out, horrified. "Mr. Murphy, you ain't selling your friends?"

"Be quiet, Belle!" her father said.

"But—"

"That's enough!"

"It's all right, Bert. It's only natural she'll be upset," Mr. Murphy said kindly. "She's always loved me elephants, haven't you, Belle?" He put his arm around her and explained, "I can't help meself, lass, and that's the truth of it. I'll not be finding another job in a hurry, not at my age. And it's a good circus they're going to, else I'd not have done it, no matter what. They'll be well looked after. Don't make it harder for me, eh?"

She shook her head. "Which two are going?" she asked in a small voice. "Not—not Tessie?"

"No, bless you," Mr. Murphy said, smiling at her. "I'll not sell our fat darling, never you fear. She's been with me since I was a boy. We've grown old together, Tessie and me. I'll never be parting with her."

Belle smiled at him, reassured.

But later, when she and Charlie went out into the yard, they were followed by the farmer's little boy, a sturdy child of six, with hair the color of his father's hay. He was always hanging around them, as if he hoped they might suddenly jump through balloons, or do a high-wire walk on his mother's washing line.

"Do you know why?" he said. "Do you know why he won't be parting from the big 'un?"

"Because he loves her."

"No, it isn't! T'isn't that at all. *I* know why. What'll you give me if I tell you?"

"A thump on your ear," Charlie said, guessing uneasily that it was something they would rather not know. Belle told him to shut up.

"Tell me, Johnny. Come on, there's a sweetheart," she wheedled. "Tell me." But he only grinned and looked knowing.

"Oh, you're silly. You're just making it up. You don't know nothing," she said, changing her tactics.

He was young enough to fall for this.

"I do know! I do! I heard them," he said, jumping up and down. "He can't get rid of the big 'un. She's too old . . ."

"She's not."

"And she's got them ugly scars on her ear. Nobody'd want her, not with them scars."

He spoke in all innocence. He had not seen the circus children since last winter and did not know about Belle's accident. So he could not understand why Charlie grabbed hold of him furiously, holding his arms so tight that it hurt.

"Shall I knock his head off, Belle?"

For a moment she was silent, and the little boy, thinking she was seriously considering it, began to whimper. Then she shook her head.

"No. Let's drown him in the duck pond."

They carried him off between them, while he squealed and wriggled, and swung him backward and forward over the muddy water's edge. He was giggling now. He liked the circus children, even though they sometimes played rough, and did not believe they would throw him in. He was right. They set him down safely on the grass.

"Do it again! Drown me again," he pleaded, but they shook their heads and went off together, saying it was no good, they'd just remembered he could swim.

During the first two weeks at Goosebeak Farm, the various bits and pieces of their painted world were packed up, driven away, sold, or burned. Two weeks of good-byes, as the artistes departed in ones and two, gloomily wishing each other luck. Two weeks of washing and ironing and packing, of having the backs of their necks scrubbed, their manners and their grammar examined, and found wanting . . .

"Don't say 'ain't,' Belle," her mother said crossly, as they sat over their tea. "How many times have I told you? You don't want your Auntie May to think you haven't been brought up proper, just because you're circus. Look at Charlie, now, you don't hear him saying 'ain't.' "

This earned Charlie a dark scowl from Belle. Mrs. Marriot went on to make things worse. "Perhaps if you'd worked as hard as he does, my girl, Mr. Schneider would've offered *you* a job at Christmas."

"He did, so there! He offered me a star billing!" Belle shouted. Seeing this lie was not believed, she added for good measure, "I hate you!" and rushed from the room.

"I shouldn't have said that," said Mrs. Marriot.

"Shall I go after her?"

"No. Best leave it. She'll want to cry, and she won't like to be caught at it. She's a prickly little puss, is our Belle. Still, I shouldn't have said that."

Charlie agreed with her but silently. Auntie Annie had a biting tongue: she was always apologizing for the wounds it inflicted, as if it were a fierce dog, quite beyond her control. Uncle Bert was different, a calm, easygoing man who walked away from arguments, saying it didn't do for a knife-throwing act to quarrel. "Don't you provoke me, Annie," he'd say, "or my hand might slip tonight and you wouldn't like that. Don't want to end up like a sliced loaf, do you?" And she'd smile and catch her tongue between her teeth. They were very fond of each other, so close that sometimes Belle and Charlie felt left out.

"I wonder what Mr. Schneider did say to her," Mrs. Marriot said now. "Do you know, Charlie?"

"No."

"She told me to mind my own business when I asked. My mother would've slapped me silly if I'd spoken to her like that. I thought of asking the Great Schneider himself, but then . . . She'd have told us soon enough if it had been anything nice. Poor Belle." She sighed, looking gloomily at the bikini in her hands, onto which she was sewing scarlet sequins. "She's a funny girl. D'you know what she said to me this morning, Charlie?"

"No."

"She asked me if I wore red so the blood wouldn't show if anything went wrong. As if Bert would ever miss! Never so much as grazed me in twenty years! Poor kid, she's lost her nerve, that's the trouble. Ever since the accident . . . Oh, Charlie, I wish we didn't have to leave you both behind. But there, we were lucky to get the chance of a job, the way things are."

She paused, looking so unhappy that Charlie said quickly, "We'll be all right."

She blinked and sniffed and smiled, all at the same time. "Yes, of course. I'm just being silly. Where's my hanky? May's very nice, you know. She offered to have you when she heard Peachem's had gone bust. It

wasn't me that asked. Well, I might've hinted a bit.
. . . Do you remember her, Charlie?"

"I think so." He had a dim memory of a tall lady,
thin, neat, dressed in gray. He had thought she was
an inspector, come to check up on the number of
hours the kids had worked, and had been surprised
when she kissed him.

"Who's she?" he had whispered to Belle, when the
lady had gone on—she seemed to be kissing everyone.
"Our new auntie," Belle had said. "Uncle George has
gone and married her. We're to have bubbly, kids and
all."

"Very much the lady, she was," Mrs. Marriot went
on. "Not one of us. Soon persuaded your poor Uncle
George to leave the circus, said she couldn't bear to
see him on that dangerous trapeze. Bought a sweetshop in Worthing. And what happens? He goes and
falls downstairs and breaks his neck! Not used to
stairs, you see. Ladders, yes, and ropes, but not stairs.
It just goes to show. You're better off where you belong. . . ." She caught sight of Charlie's face and
added quickly, "Charlie, I shouldn't have said that! I
didn't mean. . . . It's not as if you and Belle will be
out for good. Just till you get yourselves educated.
And May's very kind. She used to send you presents,
remember?"

He nodded. They had been terrible presents; fluffy
pink rabbits and plastic ducks and picture books
about elves, chosen for a baby he felt he had never
been. Presents which, if opened carelessly in front of
the other boys, had always led to jeers and fights.

"I'm sure you'll get on fine," Mrs. Marriot was saying, cheerful again. She was always an optimist, riding her troubles like horses. "It's a hard life," she was fond of saying. "We all have to take a few knocks. Doesn't do us any harm."

Charlie, watching her as she tried the effect of a silver sequin against the scarlet ones, thought, Her head's full of America and her new job. She's forgotten us already.

So he was surprised when she told him she had arranged for them to have a vacation on the farm, after she and Uncle Bert had gone. Just for two weeks, before they went on to Auntie May's.

"It was Belle wanted it," she said. "Says you've never had a proper holiday. I didn't like to refuse her, poor kid, when she's feeling so low. What do you think, Charlie? Would you like it?"

He hesitated, hating the idea. The farm depressed him now, with all their friends gone; the empty beds in his room, the yellow oblongs on the grass where the trailers had stood, the deserted stalls that had once held the circus horses, the Liberties, High School, and Rosinbacks. Except for themselves and the farm people, there was only Mr. Murphy left now, Mr. Murphy and his Tessie, both looking grayer and more worried each day. Charlie longed to be gone. Then he thought of Belle. Belle hiding behind her hair, frightened of new people, an aunt she hardly remembered, neighboring children who would point and whisper, "What's that on her face?"

So he said loyally, "Yes. That'd be great."

Mrs. Marriot smiled and told him that he was a good boy, that she and Uncle Bert looked on him as their son. . . .

"And you will take care of Belle, won't you, Charlie?"

"Yes," he said, "I'll always take care of Belle."

His words rang in his head for some time after he had said them, a rash promise, one he should never have made.

6

That night, Charlie dreamed he was back in the big top, smoothing footprints out of the sawdust with a rake. There were the small prints of children, the big-booted ones of clowns, and huge elephant tracks like cracked dinner plates.

"Look at me!" called a voice, high above him. "Charlie, look at me!"

He tilted his head and saw Belle, standing on the platform by the high wire, laughing down at him. Little fool! Showing off again.

"No! Don't!" he shouted. "Come down, Belle. Don't be stupid."

They were not allowed up there. A thousand times they had been told: Never, never touch the apparatus without permission. *Never*. It's as much as your life is worth!

Belle tossed her head.

"I can do it! I can do anything," she said, and be-gan walking out into space. He could see her feet in their soft shoes curving around the wire, her arms held out to balance her, the pale underside of her chin . . .

"Come down, Belle!" he cried, terrified. "Come down at once!" And as if he had ill-wished her, she was falling, down . . . down . . . down . . .

He sat up with a jerk, his mind full of blood and sawdust, but there was only the dark room and the empty beds on either side of him. He shivered and hugged the blankets closer. Why did he always dream it that way? It had not ended like that. Belle was not dead.

He lay awake, staring into the dark, remembering . . . Belle's arms thrashing the air as if she were try-ing to fly. Belle falling, twisting her body in midair and catching hold of the wire with her hands. Swing-ing like a pendulum above his head while he watched in terror.

He could hardly remember climbing the ladder, his face wet with tears, expecting any moment to see her body rush past him to the sawdust below. No harness, no safety net.

But when he reached the platform, she was still there, hanging limply like washing on a line. She had been trying to swing herself up so that she could catch the wire with her feet, but could not manage it. Her hands must have been raw. Charlie had grasped the rail tightly and leaned out from the platform as far as he dared, stretching out his arm.

She was too far away.

"I can't reach you!" he shouted desperately. "You'll have to come nearer!"

"I can't move. I can't."

"Yes, you can!" he screamed at her. "You're the one who can do anything. Come on. Come on!"

And she'd moved her poor bruised hands along the wire, one after another, until she was near enough for him to grab her wrist. Even then he was afraid; his hands were wet and slippery with sweat, no rosin, no chalk . . . he should have rubbed them in the sawdust . . . too late now.

"I'm going to swing you toward me," he said. "Can you grab hold of something?"

She had nodded. Oh, she'd been brave enough. Even when the edge of the platform caught her cheek, ripping it open, she had bitten back her cry and managed to catch hold of a strut, taking her weight off Charlie's arm. Then, when they were safe back in the ring, with her blood staining the sawdust at their feet and a groom rushing in, exclaiming in horror, she had smiled and said faintly, "Why, Charlie, you're a hero. You saved my life."

He had been a hero for a whole week. People had kissed him, hugged him, shaken him by the hand, and drunk to his health. Then Belle had come back from the hospital with a livid scar across her left cheek and a new, uncertain look in her eyes. The other children had been kind to her, in their way.

"You poor thing. How can you bear it? You were so pretty before, and now . . . Poor old Belle!" Lily

Reeves had kept saying, until Charlie had thumped her and had his ears boxed for hitting a girl.

Then he was back to being the old Charlie again, a boy more ready to use his fists than his tongue. People forgot he was a hero and treated him with the usual disrespect, making him fetch and carry, and cuffing him when they felt like it. True, Auntie Annie remembered, but only, he felt, when it suited her.

"I'll never forget you saved her life, Charlie," she'd say, her eyes moist with sentiment. "Never! My poor little Belle. It makes me feel better about leaving her. I know I can count on you to look after her." As if, by saving Belle's life, Charlie were now responsible for her forever.

"It's not fair," he muttered, punching his pillow for want of a better target. "Why should I? Belle's older than me." (Only three weeks, but hadn't she let him know it in the days before her accident, when she was still the young star. Vain, bossy, lording it over them all!)

But then he remembered how she had comforted him in the early days, when he was small and clumsy, teased by the other children and shouted at by the trainer. One day she had found him crying, frightened that Auntie Annie and Uncle Bert would send him away because he was no good.

"What's the matter?" she had asked. "Is it the other boys? Hit them if they're horrid. Hard. On the nose." (Advice which he had later taken too much to heart.)

When he had confessed the shameful truth, that he

was hopeless, that he'd never catch up with the other kids, she had hugged him and said, "It ain't true. You can do it, Charlie. I'll show you. I'll help you. If you work at it, you can be as good as anyone. Well, except me, of course."

And he knew he must always love her and look after her as best he could. But, tossing on his bed, he wished he were older, fearing uneasily that his best would not be enough.

Three days later, Mr. and Mrs. Marriot left Goosebeak Farm. Belle had wanted to go to London with them, to see them off at the airport, but her mother had said that she hated long good-byes.

"Hanging around for hours, having time to get miserable. It'd only make me cry and spoil my mascara." She blinked her eyes as if to show how thick and black her lashes were and what a pity it would be to spoil them. She did not look as sorry to go as she should have. All dressed up for the journey in tight pink trousers and a white satin blouse, her bleached hair tied back with a scarlet ribbon, Mrs. Marriot looked in a party rather than a departing mood. "Good-bye, Belle darling," she said, beaming. "Be a good girl. Look after Charlie. . . ." Above Belle's head she caught Charlie's eye and winked, as if to say, "You know who's really got to do the looking after, don't you?" Then she hugged Belle. "There, give your mum a big kiss. Chin up and keep smiling, that's circus. Where's my bag gone? Charlie, have you seen . . . oh, there it is! Come on, Bert, we don't want to miss the train. Bye, Belle! Bye, Charlie! Take care. . . ."

"Good luck! See you sometime!" Belle called.

The car drove off down the muddy lane and they watched it out of sight, waving. Then it was gone. Twelve years, thought Belle, twelve years she had lived with her mum and dad, slept in the same trailer, listened to their snores through the thin partition when she woke at night. Twelve years of being kissed and cuffed by her mother, comforted by her father—and now it was over. When they met again, she would be different; older, educated by a new school, turned by Auntie May into . . . what? A young lady, perhaps, speaking in a mincing little voice, never saying "ain't," wearing neat gray dresses and washing the back of her neck every day. They wouldn't recognize her. Come to think of it, she wouldn't recognize herself.

She didn't feel unhappy, exactly. She didn't know what she felt. Just blank. They were alone now, she and Charlie, alone in an in-between time; the circus world gone, the suburbs and the sweetshop still to come. Oh, well, might as well make the best of it while it lasted.

She glanced at Charlie and saw that he was watching her uneasily. Wondering if I'm going to cry, she thought. For a moment she considered putting on a poor-little-orphan act, all wet and wistful, to embarrass Charlie and get Mrs. Thorpe running around, offering hankies and buttered scones, with herself the center of attention. But she decided against it. It wasn't her style: she was a secret weeper. She had done her crying last night, face pressed into a damp pillow. So she gave Charlie her widest smile and said cheerfully, "That's that. What shall we do now?"

Mrs. Thorpe, hearing her, thought, How heartless children are! You love them, work for them, worry about them, and then it's "Good-bye, Mum. Good-bye, Dad. See you sometime," and they walk away laughing.

7

Mr. Murphy was in the elephant shed.

"What are we going to do, Tessie, old girl?" he asked, popping a piece of apple into her soft mouth. "Over three million out of work, they say. Time for old men and old elephants to retire, eh? Would you like that?"

The elephant rumbled softly, as if agreeing.

And for sure, they could both do with a rest, Mr. Murphy thought. He hadn't been feeling himself lately. "You don't look well, Danny," his sister had said, last time they met. "You need someone to look after you. Move in with me, I could do with a bit of company. Been a bit lonesome on me own."

He was fond of Maureen. His sister, once at the top of a pyramid of acrobats, had retired five years ago to a council flat in Worthing. "There's always room for you, Danny," she had said. But not, of course, for his

Tessie. "We aren't allowed pets, not in our block. Not even a canary. Though I won't say I haven't heard the odd cheep coming from behind closed doors. Nor the odd meow, neither; though there's not a word I'd let slip about it to anyone but you. What's a few fleas compared to loneliness? But I'm sorry, there's limits, Danny. I can't do with an elephant in me kitchen. It's not a thing you can hide easy."

True enough.

"Got to think of something, Tess," he said, taking the elephant's trunk out of his pocket, where it had been searching hopefully for another titbit. "Can't stay here forever. Mrs. Thorpe's got it in for you, lass. She don't like elephants no more, silly woman. Wants your shed to store turnips in, or something. You and me's got to move on. . . ."

"Ain't you found nothing yet, Mr. Murphy?"

It was Belle, coming silently into the shed. She moved like a shadow in her sneakers. He never heard her coming nowadays. Getting a bit deaf, most likely. Talking to himself, too. Going to pieces.

He wondered how much she'd overheard. He didn't want to upset her, the poor little kid, with her face reflecting his own fears like a mirror. She loved that old elephant as much as he did.

"We was just talking, Tessie and me," he said, smiling at her. "And we've decided we're going to retire."

"Retire?"

"We've got our plans fixed. A small zoo for Tessie, with me in a cottage at the gate, so I can visit easy. Maybe earn the odd penny helping to muck out.

They'll be glad of a hand, no doubt, and that way Tessie won't get lonely."

He did not tell her that he had already written to several zoos, with no success. With the price of feed and vet's bills rocketing, no one wanted an old, scarred circus elephant, even as a gift. But the truth was too cold for children, you had to dress it up a little. How could he say that he often woke up, in the small, dark hours, his heart on the trot, remembering his sister's words. . . . "You've got to face it, Danny," Maureen had said, "you'll not get another job at your age. You'll have to have that poor old elephant put down. There's no way you can support her on a pension."

No, he couldn't tell Belle that. So he told her instead about his dreams of a small zoo, with a cottage at the gate, till he almost came to believe in them himself. A garden where he could grow roses. Carrots and apples, too, to take to Tessie. His sister would come and live with him and cook his supper. . . . "And when I'm back from visiting me fat friend, there'll be hot, buttered crumpets and tea in a brown pot, and we'll yarn about old times. How does that sound, Belle?"

"Fantastic."

Something in the way she said it made him look at her sharply, but she had turned away and was fondling the elephant's scarred ear. He could not see her face. They were too sharp, these kids. They grew up quickly nowadays, poor little devils.

He said, to change the subject, "Heard from your mum and dad yet?"

"We got a cable, saying they'd arrived safely. It's too soon for a letter."

"Of course, it's only three days. Enjoying your vacation, are you?"

"Not bad," she said, shrugging. "Mr. Thorpe let us both have a turn driving the tractor yesterday. And today he showed us how to milk the cows. Me and Charlie had a cow each." She laughed, glancing back at him. "Charlie's kicked the bucket, and there was milk all over. I never seen his feet so white before—nor his face so red!"

"I thought it was all done electric?"

"Yes. But Mr. Thorpe says you can't never tell when you're going to have a power cut. And it's something for us to do. Funny, ain't it? We was always having to work, never no time to ourselves, except when we . . ."

"When you sneaked off on the sly, eh? I know."

"Yeah, well, now we got all the time we want and"—she screwed up her face—"I dunno. It don't seem so much fun, somehow."

"And that's a fine thought for a man about to retire, I must say! Any more words of cheer for me, Belle? Anything else to hearten an old man who's hanging his cap up?"

She smiled, shaking her head. Her heavy yellow hair swung back, showing the long, ragged scar on her left cheek. He could not stop himself from glancing at it and though he looked immediately away again, she had noticed. Her hand went quickly up to pull her hair back into place, and she flushed.

Oh, hell, poor kid! Should he say nothing? But someone ought to coax her out into the open. She couldn't go around with half a face for the rest of her life.

"Now, Belle, me darling," he began, but the pity showed in his voice and immediately she stiffened. Her one visible eye glared at him, and she sidled toward the open doors. Oh, he was grown old and clumsy. Losing his touch. There's times you can gentle a young lion, and times you'll get your head bitten off. Best change course . . .

"That's right, run away just when I'm after asking you a favor," he said plaintively, as she reached the door.

She turned, looking doubtful.

"What favor?"

He'd offered to help Mr. Thorpe repair some fencing tomorrow, he told her. Take all day, most likely, and there was poor old Tessie. He didn't like to leave her shut up by herself for so long, not when she was still missing her friends.

"No telling what mischief she'd get into," he said, looking around the large, dilapidated shed, with its high, cracked windows and chinks of light showing here and there through the boards. "Wouldn't take much to have this place down about her ears. Only got to lean a little."

"I'll look after her!" Belle said, her face brightening, as he had known it would. "Me and Charlie. We'll take her for a walk. She'll like that."

"No going down to the village to show off," he warned her. "Keep well away from the roads, we don't want her frightening some driver into the ditch."

"No. I promise."

"And not near the house, mind. I'd as soon Mrs. Thorpe didn't catch sight of her, or she'll be after me again."

"We'll be careful."

"There's the bottom meadow, only check there's no cows in it first. Not that she'd hurt them, bless her, but if the milk comes out cheesy, it'll be our blame. We're not so welcome here anymore, that's the sad truth."

"We'll be careful, Mr. Murphy, honest," Belle said. "We've looked after her before. You can trust us."

"Yes," he said, smiling, "you've got a way with elephants, Belle. Tessie will do anything for you, I've noticed. I know she'll be all right. So I won't be fretting to come back early tomorrow."

But he *was* back early. It was not yet twelve o'clock, with the sun high and hot in the sky, when they brought him back. Charlie and Belle were leading Tessie back from the bottom meadow, where they had been playing in the stream, when they heard someone shouting. They looked around. Mr. Thorpe and another man were coming slowly, heavily across the grass, carrying between them a stretcher, on which lay something still and dark.

Mr. Thorpe shouted again, and now they could make out the words, "Run on ahead! Tell them to ring for an ambulance! Quick!"

Charlie turned and ran. Belle could hear his feet clattering as he reached the paved yard and then his voice calling, high-pitched, and a door banging. . . . She could see now whom they were carrying on the stretcher. It was Mr. Murphy. She ran toward them.

Mr. Murphy was lying on his back, his nose pointing to the sky, his eyes shut. From his mouth came odd, harsh, snoring noises that frightened her.

"Is he . . ." she began, but Mr. Thorpe said sharply, "Get that damn animal away!"

For Tessie had followed her and was stretching out her trunk toward her old friend, as if puzzled by the strange sounds he was making.

"Back, Tessie, back," Belle said, pushing against Tessie's cheek, trying to turn her. But the elephant had sensed something was wrong. Her ears came forward uneasily, and she began swinging her trunk from side to side, her small, pouched eyes fixed with anxious love on the unconscious man.

"She won't do him no harm," Belle said.

"For God's sake! She'll have him off the stretcher in a minute!"

"Stand! Tessie, stand!" Belle commanded shrilly, pushing the elephant's trunk away from Mr. Murphy and getting between her and the stretcher. For a moment she felt frightened, suddenly doubting her power over the great, gray colossus that loomed above her, three tons of worried elephant wanting to go forward, with only Belle in the way. Mustn't let fear show. Fear was catching. And it was only Tessie, whom she had known as long as she could remember.

"Steady, old girl," she said, keeping her voice low and calm. "Mustn't let Mr. Murphy think you've forgotten all he's taught you. That's better. Now, right turn!" She put her hand behind Tessie's trunk and tried to lead her away. It was like trying to move a mountain. The elephant stood planted, her legs like trees, her heavy head turning to watch the men carrying Mr. Murphy away. But she no longer tried to follow.

Belle felt her eyes blur with tears. "Poor old Tess," she said. "You're worried, ain't you? But it'll be all right, you'll see. Mr. Murphy ain't going to die. He *ain't!*"

She kept talking, soothing the great animal as they both watched their friend being carried into the house. Only when the door had shut did Belle try again to lead the elephant back to the shed. Tessie came with her willingly now, though she was still uneasy, her ears moving like ragged leaves in the wind. Taking her into the shed, Belle fixed the leather-covered shackle onto her hind leg, which tethered her by a chain to an iron ring in the ground. Then she gave her water and left her feed within easy reach.

"I'll be back, Tessie, don't worry," she said. "I must go and see how . . ."

She could not finish her sentence. She was shivering now and could no longer trust her voice. So she shut the door behind her, hearing, as she did so, the wailing of an ambulance in the distance.

8

Mr. Murphy had had a mild stroke, but there was every hope that, with good nursing and rest, he would make a complete recovery. So Mr. Thorpe told them when he returned from the hospital, to eat his warmed-up, dried-up lunch at the kitchen table.

"Grandpa had a stroke last year," Johnny Thorpe said. "And now he walks funny—hup bonk, hup bonk, hup bonk . . ." The small boy capered grotesquely around the table, crying, "Watch me! I'm Grandpa!"

"Stop it, Johnny!" his mother said sharply.

"Can we go and see him?" Belle asked.

"Not for the moment," Mr. Thorpe told her. "No visitors allowed, apart from family. His sister's coming up today."

"That's nice," Mrs. Thorpe said. "That'll be a comfort to him. There's nothing like your own family."

"Does he talk funny?" Johnny asked. "Grandpa did. Grandpa went wah, wah, wah . . . ow!" he finished shrilly as his mother slapped him.

"That's enough from you," she said angrily, and then turned to Belle. "Don't worry, dear. He'll be all right, I'm sure. It's wonderful how they get over it. You should see Dad now, fit as he's ever been, except for this little limp. . . ."

"Hup bonk, hup bonk."

"Out!" she shouted furiously, and the small boy fled.

The Thorpes smiled apologetically at Belle and Charlie. Told them not to take any notice of Johnny ("You know what they're like at that age"). No need to worry. Mr. Murphy was going to be all right. . . . Their voices poured over Belle like golden syrup.

It was hot in the farmhouse kitchen. Sunlight lay in yellow slices on the table, and the air smelled richly of casserole and coalite. By the window a fly was buzzing: it was the very sound of summer. Belle looked across the table at Charlie, who smiled at her, his mouth mustached with milk. He was content, lapping up the comforting words.

Perhaps there's something wrong with me, Belle thought. I can't seem to believe anyone no more. The kinder they sound, the more I worry . . .

Through the open window she could hear Johnny still chanting his verbal limping, though quietly now, as if pride compelled him to continue but discretion warned him not to be heard. Hup bonk, hup bonk. Well, at least, she thought, comforted, his grandpa is able to walk, even though with a limp. She could trust Johnny. Johnny was too young to deceive her for her own good.

"How long will Mr. Murphy be in the hospital?" she asked.

It was too early to tell, they said. "I expect Mrs. O'Hara will ring us as soon as she has any news," Mrs. Thorpe added. "She'll want to arrange to collect his things."

"Won't he be coming back here?"

"I don't know, dear. I shouldn't think so. He'll probably go straight to his sister when he leaves the hospital. He'll need looking after for a bit."

"What about Tessie?" Belle asked.

The Thorpes exchanged a quick glance, but it was not quick enough. Belle might have only one eye uncovered, but that eye was sharp. They don't like Tessie, she thought. They want to get rid of her.

"We'll look after her," she said quickly. "She won't be no trouble to you. We can do it easy, can't we, Charlie?" He nodded.

"That's very kind of you, dear," Mrs. Thorpe said. Again she glanced briefly, warningly, at her husband. She might just as well have shouted, Keep it from the children. We don't want to upset them. There's no need for them to know.

"What is it? What's going to happen to Tessie?" Belle demanded, her eyes going anxiously from one kindly deceiving face to another.

"I don't know, dear. That's up to Mrs. O'Hara now, not us. I'm sure she'll do what's best."

Don't worry. Mr. Murphy's comfortable. Mr. Murphy's as well as can be expected. Everything's going to be all right. They were told this every day, when they asked, but Belle was uneasy.

"I think we should go and see him ourselves," she said to Charlie as they stood watching Tessie stuffing herself happily with hay. "We could say we're relatives. Only I don't trust . . . someone," she ended, having caught sight of Johnny, sitting on the fence, his ears as large and red as poppies.

"Who?" the small boy asked.

"No one you know."

"I do, then! Bet I do!"

"Oh, go away, Johnny," Belle said impatiently. "Why do you always have to follow us around? We don't want you. Shove off!"

"Or we'll set Tessie on you," said Charlie.

"And she'll squash you flat."

"Then your mum will fold you up and keep you in a drawer."

"All in the dark."

The small boy's face crumpled, for there was an unkind note to the teasing. He climbed down from the fence and said with childish dignity, trying not to cry, "I was going to tell you something important, but I won't now."

Belle was immediately ashamed. "I'm sorry, Johnny," she said quickly. "We didn't mean to be beastly. Only we're worried, see, and that makes people horrid. Would you like to feed Tessie an apple?"

"No."

He was hurt. It took Belle all her charm and two toffees to appease him. Even then she hesitated to ask him what he'd been about to tell them, in case he suspected the motives for her sudden kindness had been mixed.

Johnny had a gift for eavesdropping. Being small, he was often hidden by a table or behind an armchair. He could walk past a window, and only the top tufts of his hair would be visible, easily mistaken for dried grass. If anyone could tell her what was going on, Johnny could. And did: he could never keep his illicit knowledge to himself for long.

"That woman's been and gone," he said.

"What woman?"

"Mrs. O' summat—you know, his sister. She took his things away."

"Mrs. O'Hara? When? She hasn't left already?"

He nodded.

"But we wanted to see her! Why didn't you come and tell us she was here?"

"I was listening," he said simply.

Belle pushed past him and raced back to the farmhouse; thundered into the kitchen, which was empty; shouted for Mrs. Thorpe, who didn't answer.

Charlie and Johnny had followed her in. "Where's your mum?" she asked the small boy.

"Dunno."

She thumped the table angrily with her fist, making the teacups rattle and a little milk slop out of a jug.

"I see she had time for tea," she said bitterly.

"They might have sent for us. They knew we'd be with Tessie."

"They said, better not," Johnny explained, watching her curiously with his round blue eyes. "They said you'd only make a fuss about the elephant."

"What about her?"

"The slaughterhouse people are coming for her on Monday." He giggled uneasily, looking at them from beneath his pale eyelashes. "Won't she make a lot of cat's meat?"

9

When Charlie woke up, he was conscious of a shadow lying over the bright day like a bad dream. Then he remembered. Tessie! Not all their pleading last night had been any good; on Monday the slaughterhouse truck was coming to take her away.

"It's murder!" Belle had shrieked. "She can't do it! I won't let her! Tessie ain't hers. I'll go and tell Mr. Murphy. . . ."

Mr. Murphy was very ill. Did she want to upset him? Did she want to spoil his recovery? Wasn't his life more important than any animal's? And had she no thought for Mrs. O'Hara, frantic with worry about her brother, wanting to have him home with her so she could nurse him back to health . . .

"Be reasonable, Belle," Mr. Thorpe had said. "How can they keep an elephant in a council flat?"

"Tessie's to go to a zoo! Mr. Murphy told me!" It

was then they learned that Mr. Murphy had already written to several zoos and been refused.

"What could he do? He had to agree. These are hard times," Mr. Thorpe had said. Everyone was always telling them that. These are hard times, bad times, you chose to be born at the wrong moment, you've missed out on the good old days . . . As if they'd been careless, arriving too late for some party.

It was no use trying to go back to sleep. He had better go in and see if Belle was awake. Poor Belle, it was worse for her. She adored old Tessie; there was a bond between the scarred girl and the scarred elephant. He hated the thought of her unhappiness, dreaded finding her sunk into the deep misery that had made her say once, "You shouldn't have saved my life, Charlie. You shouldn't have bothered."

But when he opened her door, he found the room empty. She was already up. Where? Not in the kitchen, where Mrs. Thorpe greeted him coldly, her patience having been strained by yesterday's scenes. The elephant shed? No. She had been there, for Tessie was outside, in the fenced-in patch of dried mud, peacefully eating some greens, and her tub was filled with fresh water. But there was no Belle. Charlie began to get worried.

"Belle!" he shouted. "Belle!"

He looked out over the sunlit fields, but he could not see her. The stream? Surely it was not deep enough to drown in?

He went racing over the grass toward the bottom meadow, and then he saw them, Belle and Johnny, sitting on the low branch of a tree, deep in talk. Belle was smiling. As he watched she put out a hand and ruffled the small boy's hair.

"That's clever, Johnny," she said. "You *have* got a good memory. I bet you're top of the class at school."

She was up to something. She was speaking in her buttering-up voice, the one she used to charm the money out of a sucker's pocket, after a private show. Puzzled, but not wanting to spoil her game, whatever it was, Charlie walked back to the elephant shed and sat on the fence outside, waiting for her.

It was five minutes before she came, her face alight with triumph.

"Barstow's," she said.

"What?"

"The slaughterhouse. Barstow's of Summaton. I can look them up in the directory. They ain't planning to do it here—I suppose a live elephant's easier to move than a dead one. I'm going to ring them up and put them off. I'm good at doing voices. How's this?" She deepened her voice, and it could have been the farmer's wife speaking. "Is that Barstow's? This is Mrs. Thorpe of Goosebeak Farm. I'm calling to cancel the arrangements about the elephant."

Charlie's heart sank. "They'll only call back to find out why the truck didn't come," he said. "It won't do any good."

"I'm not thick, Charlie. I've got a plan."

Her eye was shining, her face as bright as the summer morning. This was not the sad girl who had lost her nerve. This was Belle as she had once been, the young circus star who had walked so lightly, so easily, over the low wire that she'd fixed her eyes on impossible heights, looking up to where the high wire, the forbidden wire, gleamed in the lofty shadows of the big top. "I can do anything," she had said. But she had fallen.

"What plan?" Charlie asked, feeling horribly uneasy.

She hesitated, looking sly.

"Promise to help me?" she asked.

"Without knowing what I'm letting myself in for? Come off it, Belle! I'm not that daft!"

"Swear, then," she demanded. "Swear on the Old Gent." Her face grew solemn as she evoked the strange circus oath of secrecy, an oath heavy with time and usage, though its meaning was lost. Neither of them knew who the Old Gent was or why he should be so terrible. Some people said he was the devil, others that he was a man in evening dress who appeared in a ringside seat before every fatal accident. Whatever the truth, it was a vow no circus child would break lightly. But Charlie did not hesitate. He'd never sneak on Belle anyhow. She should have known that.

"May the Old Gent take me if I ever tell," he said.

Belle led him into the elephant shed, where none of the farm people would dare follow, being foolishly afraid of Tessie. They sat down on some straw in a dark corner, close as conspirators. Even then, she kept looking around uneasily, as if expecting to see the sun shining through a large red ear, pressed to one of the many chinks between the boards. When she spoke, her voice was so soft and breathy that Charlie hoped he was not hearing her right.

For it was a crazy plan, as full of gaps as the shed they sat in. Kidnap Tessie? Oh, sure! Sneak her out of the farm and take her secretly, unseen (an elephant, mind you), through Yald Forest to Blanstock Safari Park on the other side. Some thirty miles as the crow flies, lucky bird; more like a hundred for two weary children and an elderly elephant, dodging the summer hikers and riders and campers around every tree.

"Blanstock's the first place Mr. Murphy would have tried," he objected. "They've probably already turned her down."

"It's easy to say no by letter. But once she's in there, once we've gotten her inside . . ."

"How? Do we wrap her up in brown paper, knock on their door, and say we've brought them a big present?"

"Leave it to me," Belle said, looking cross and stubborn. "Just trust me, Charlie."

He was silent, knowing it was no good trying to make her see reason when she was in this mood. "Look after Belle," his aunt had said. How? Tie her up and lock her in a cupboard until Tuesday? Look at her now, her eye shining like a star, all excited about her silly plan. Didn't she know what it would mean? That it was no matter of being slapped and sent to bed without supper, when they were caught. . . .

"You realize they'll have the whole police force after us?" he said.

But she shook her head. "They won't know nothing about it. None of them. They'll all think we're somewhere else. I've got it worked out. Listen . . ."

So he listened while she spun her thin, intricate web in his ear. No spider would have owned such a ramshackle affair, full of tangles and loose ends and holes big enough to put a camel through.

"But, Belle," he kept saying, and she would wave away his objections with a thin hand.

"We'll travel by night and hide up by day," she said.

"It's impossible. . . ."

"Everything sounds impossible till it's been done. Nobody'd ever have done the triple twist somersault if they'd listened to you. Do you want poor Tessie to die?"

"No, but . . ."

"Just give it a try, that's all I'm asking. I'll *never* ask you for nothing again, I promise. I'll help you with your practice. I'll mend your beastly clothes when you've been fighting. I'll stick up for you at that horrid new school. I'll be an angel. *Please,* Charlie!"

He did not stand a chance. He could feel himself weakening.

"We'd need money," he said, on the edge on his last ditch. "We'd need a lot of things, sleeping bags, ground cloths . . ."

"We got money. We got the fund."

The fund. A hundred and seven pounds. "But that was for your face," he said. "That was for Harley Street."

"This is more important."

He was suddenly angry, thinking of the hours they had worked at their private shows, the risks they had taken, the hard, dull slog of saving, going without everything so that Belle could have a pretty face again. And she could give it up just like that.

"Oh, it's easy to say so now," he said crossly. "But what about later? Do you think they'll let you wear your hair all over your face at our new school? No chance! They'll make you tie it back. How will you like that?"

"I don't care!"

"Tie it back, then. Go on. Let's see your silly scar."

"If I do, then will you help me?"

He hesitated, seeing nothing but disaster in her ridiculous plan, too many things to go wrong, landing them in bad trouble with everyone. Aunt May, the police, his aunt and uncle fetched back from America —and he himself losing his chance with Mr. Schneider, for what circus would take on a boy who had pinched an elephant?

"Will you, Charlie?" she asked again.

"Yes," he said helplessly.

"Got a piece of string?"

He fumbled in his pockets: two pennies; a dirty tissue; chewing gum; an old shoelace. . . . He handed it to her and watched her tie the long, fair hair back from her face.

Then she turned to him, tilting her head so that the light from the small, high windows fell on her cheek. "A penny for the peepshow," she said bitterly.

He looked at her steadily. Her face still seemed cut in half, one side white where it had been hidden from the sun, one brown. The scar had healed, its ugly, livid color gone. It ran from the hairline, missing her eye, right down to her chin. The left side of her mouth was pulled up a little, so that she appeared to be smiling, though her eyes were miserable.

"It's not so bad," he said. "Dunno what you've been making such a fuss about. Now, this plan of ours . . ."

He saw her face light up at the word *ours* and felt guilty, knowing he was counting on things going wrong at the beginning, before they had gone too far. Oh, there'd still be a fight, of course, but no worse than he and Belle had weathered in the past. But once in Yald Forest—it was things going on behind his back he was afraid of. The police, the telephone calls, the headlines in the newspapers—HAVE YOU SEEN THESE CHILDREN OR THIS ELEPHANT? No, it mustn't come to that.

"But I won't cheat," he told himself, soothing his conscience. "I'll do my best. It won't be my fault then."

10

Well, it was done now. The first step was taken, and there was no going back. That afternoon, while Mr. Thorpe was out mending his fences and Mrs. Thorpe was driving Johnny to a birthday party, the farmer's office was taken over. His chair was sat in, his telephone used, his wife's voice borrowed.

The man at Barstow's did not seem suspicious. "Mrs. Thorpe? Ah, yes, good afternoon, madam. That's the elephant, isn't it?" he said. "We have it down on our books for collection on Monday. . . . Oh. Oh, I see. You want to cancel it altogether?" He was obviously disappointed, sounding like an executioner who had been promised a queen, only to have her snatched away at the last moment, her head still on her shoulders. Barstow's would never make history now. It was back to the dull routine of sheep and cattle for them. "I wish you could have let us know sooner, madam," he said coldly. "We'd already arranged for the vet. . . . Yes. I see. I suppose it can't be helped. Very well, madam."

Belle's hand was trembling when she put down the telephone. She looked at Charlie, and they exchanged nervous smiles.

Outside in the yard again, they sat on a bench in the sun, rehearsing their next act until they were letter-perfect; then falling silent, with the familiar fluttering beginning in their stomachs. It was like waiting to go into the ring.

Belle's face felt naked. Her hand kept going up to her left cheek, her fingers touching the scar briefly.

"What's the matter? Does it itch?" Charlie asked when she'd done it for the sixth time.

"No."

"It wasn't so bad, was it? At lunch?"

She did not answer. He would never guess how she had felt, walking into the kitchen with her hair tied back, seeing Mrs. Thorpe's eyes go to her cheek, then dart away again. Suppose I'll have to get used to it, she thought, people's eyes jumping away from my face like it was something nasty on the pavement. My eyes are all right, and my nose, even my mouth, ain't too bad, but it don't make any difference. It's my scar they look at and then wish they hadn't! Nobody'll ever look me straight in the face no more.

Except Johnny. Johnny was too young for tact. He had come right up to her and stared.

"Boy, what a big scar." His voice had expressed only interest, not pity. "I've got a scar on my knee," he'd said, showing it to her. "I had to have three stitches. How many did you have?"

"Five hundred and fifty-five," she said, exaggerating wildly.

He was impressed. "How did you get it?" he'd asked, almost enviously, as if he'd have liked one just as large to show off at school.

"It was a tiger done it," she invented. "I was cleaning his cage, see, and I slipped on the soap. Never fall down in front of tigers, Johnny, or they'll do you. They can't help themselves, poor things, it's their nature."

"Oh!" he'd breathed, his eyes and mouth round with wonder. At least there was one admirer she hadn't lost.

Then Charlie said suddenly, "She's back!" and Belle saw the car coming through the farm gates.

They ran to meet Mrs. Thorpe, putting on bright smiles like masks. They were practiced performers. No one listening to their excited voices would have guessed they were lying. Their aunt had just rung up, they told Mrs. Thorpe. Auntie May was going to take them on a canal holiday, on a barge—it would mean their leaving the farm early, but she didn't mind, did she? They did so want to go, they'd never been on a boat before. . . .

"We told Auntie May it would be all right," Belle said. "We were sure you wouldn't mind."

"Of course not, dear," Mrs. Thorpe said comfortably. To tell the truth, she'd be glad to see the back of them. All that fuss about an elephant! "I'll give your aunt a ring in a minute—"

But apparently that was not possible. Their aunt had already left, they told her. A friend was driving her up to fetch the barge, and there was no way of getting in touch with her now. But it was all arranged. Belle and Charlie were to meet the barge at Oxford on Monday. They were to catch the two thirty-five from Summaton. . . .

"*This* Monday?"

"Yes," said Belle, and watched Mrs. Thorpe from under her lashes. There was a funny look on the woman's face. Had she remembered Tessie was also going on Monday? Behind those blank blue eyes was the image of a barge slowly turning into that of an elephant? Quick, say something. Don't give her time to get suspicious.

"Auntie May suggested Saturday at first, but . . . but . . ." Belle let her voice falter and hung her head to hide her tearless eyes. "Poor old Tess, the least we can do is stay with her until . . ." Her voice trailed away, and she sniffed loudly.

"Now don't you upset yourself again," Mrs. Thorpe said anxiously.

"You know, you'd never get Tessie on that truck without us," Charlie said. "Elephants can turn funny if they take against someone. She's been acting sort of nervous lately, I dunno why. Seems to've gone off the men here. Probably blames them for taking Mr. Murphy away. Yesterday she was swinging her trunk like a sledgehammer when Mr. Thorpe went by. Scraping the ground with her foot, too. Reminded me of that time in Kent—"

"Shut up, Charlie! We're not supposed to talk about it. You know we promised."

"About what? What happened?" Mrs. Thorpe said sharply.

"Oh, nothing. Nothing much."

"Just some man made a bit of a fuss. She didn't really hurt him."

"He was only in the hospital a week."

Mrs. Thorpe looked thoroughly alarmed. "But Mr. Murphy always said she was as gentle as a lamb. . . ."

"Ah, yes, with *him,* she is," said Charlie.

"And with me," said Belle.

"But she doesn't like strangers."

"Nor trucks."

"And you'd best keep Johnny away. She don't like small boys much."

"Nor dogs."

Mrs. Thorpe looked suitably worried, and they thought they had better stop. They did not want to overdo it.

"Belle can handle her," Charlie said. "She'll do anything for Belle."

"Yes." Belle sounded sad. "I'll load her up for you. She won't be frightened with me. But I wish it were over and we were on that barge."

And she and Charlie started talking about boats and canals and locks, until Mrs. Thorpe's head spun and there was no room for suspicion left inside it.

The expected letter from America came on Saturday, two pages for Belle and two for Charlie, on thin air-mail paper that rustled in their fingers. The words were stilted and misspelled (the Marriots seldom wrote letters), but they were full of love.

"It's great here," they said. "They got it all, lions, tigers, a stagecoach, you ought to see the stagecoach galloping around the ring, with Indians after it and guns shooting, you'd love it. Puts dear old Peachem's in the shade. It's a bit big, not that we don't love it, but we miss you both. Dad keeps saying Belle would like that, can't you see Charlie in that ten-gallon hat. . . ."

The pages were hemmed with kisses. Belle and Charlie were very quiet after they had finished reading. They folded the pages carefully and put them away, not looking at each other. "Be good," the letter had ended. "Take care of yourselves. Don't do anything we wouldn't do."

11

On Monday morning at ten to eleven, an ill wind suddenly swept upon Goosebeak Farm. First Charlie came rushing in to say the cows were in the cornfield —was that all right? Only they seemed to be making a mess of it. No, *he* hadn't left the gate open, he'd just found it like that. Perhaps it had blown open. Mr. Thorpe and his cowman went off at a run, and Charlie vanished again.

Then Mrs. Thorpe, coming into her kitchen, found her big glass jug on the floor, a hundred splinters in a sea of milk, spread before the feet of an astonished cat. She swore at the cat, who leaped onto the windowsill, from where he gave her a look of affronted innocence—*he* had nothing to do with it, he had just found it like that!

Before she had time to get a cloth, Johnny ran in, barefoot, to tell her the goat had somehow gotten loose from its tether and was now in the garden, munching pansies.

"Look out! There's broken glass everywhere!" she shouted at him. "Go and put your shoes on this minute!"

"But, Mum, the goat—"

"Damn the goat!"

"Mrs. Thorpe! Mrs. Thorpe!" It was Charlie again, bursting in through the door in high excitement. "Barstow's have come for Tessie."

"Watch out for the milk!" she shrieked at him. He skidded to a halt, knocked into a chair, and fell over with it.

"That's dangerous," he said reproachfully when he'd righted himself and the chair. "You oughtn't to leave it—look, there's glass all over! Someone could cut themselves."

"I'm quite aware of that," she said, tight-lipped. "I was just going to clear it up. Tell the driver I'll be out in a minute. . . ."

"Oh, he can't wait. He's in a hurry. He wouldn't even come up the lane."

"What do you mean? Where is he?"

"Parked over there, on the main road," Charlie said, pointing through the window to where the top of a high truck was just visible above the distant hedge. "Belle's taking Tessie down now. I'd keep Johnny in, if I were you, Mrs. Thorpe. Tessie's playing up a bit."

"But I want to watch! I want to watch!" said Johnny, making a dash for the door. His mother caught him back just before he stepped into the milk and dumped him on a chair, saying furiously, "You stay there and don't move! Do you hear me? *Don't move.*"

"I just came to say good-bye," Charlie said, "and thanks for everything. I can't stop. The driver says he'll give us a lift to Summaton if we hurry."

"But Charlie, your train's not till—"

"By the way, I forgot to tell you. Did you know the goat's eating your roses?"

"Not my Golden Glory?"

"Dunno what they're called. Yellow ones. I must rush. We've already taken our luggage down. Good-bye, Mrs. Thorpe. Bye, Johnny."

"Charlie! Charlie, wait a minute!"

But he was gone. She could hear his feet thundering across the yard and down the lane.

She hesitated, her mind filled with goats and roses and broken glass. . . . Why hadn't that stupid driver brought the truck up to the farm? It was a long walk down the lane, and Johnny with no shoes on. Someone should supervise the loading of the elephant onto the truck—couldn't leave it all to the children. Still, the men from Barstow's would be there, it was their job. And what good would she be? That great lumbering creature frightened the life out of her, and they said animals could always tell. The smell of fear made them attack. Oh, why was William always out when he was needed? she thought unfairly, forgetting her husband was chasing the cows from the cornfield.

So she stood, with too many things to do, doing none of them, but staring out of the window with the

cloth in her hand, the milk on the floor, and her little
boy whining on his chair because Belle had not said
good-bye to him.

"And you shut up!" she told him crossly. "If you'd
got your shoes on, we could've gone after them.
You've only yourself to blame."

She felt uneasy, with an odd sense of having been
blown off course. . . . But they were circus children,
she comforted herself, brought up rough. They'd be
all right.

It seemed ages since Belle had stopped the truck.
Why didn't Charlie come? Had something gone
wrong? "Give me fifteen minutes," he'd said. "You
mustn't let it drive off too soon, or it'll give the show
away. Wait for my signal." It must be longer than
fifteen minutes, and she was running out of ideas. Already the driver was getting suspicious.

He had stopped with a hiss of brakes when she had
flagged him down, waving her arms wildly, her hair
flying, her mouth open in a childish cry for help. He
was an Asian, a plump, youngish man with kind,
dark eyes in a brown face. He had patted her shoulder
gently when she had leapt onto the step of the high
cab, clutched hold of his arm through the open window, and buried her face in his sleeve, sobbing noisily.
He smelled of diesel and something sweetish—was it
chocolate? The advertisements must be true, she
thought, swallowing an impulse to giggle, and truck
drivers really did eat chocolate all the time.

"What is the trouble? Try to tell me. You are safe now, my friend."

She had taken her time, gulping and sniffing and whimpering, counting the slow seconds passing in her head. The more time she could waste, the better. But she could not keep it up forever. Lily Reeves could cry at will, real tears, simply by thinking of something sad. It was a talent Belle lacked, so she kept her face hidden, resisting the finger that tried gently to raise her chin. Half opening one eye, she tried to squint at her watch, but it was too close. Out of focus, it looked like frog spawn, a black dot where the hands joined in a round gray blur.

"Are you hurt? Has someone frightened you?" the driver asked.

"No, I—uh, uh, uh! It's—uh, uh, uh!" she gulped, letting her voice rise as if climbing a ladder to hysteria.

He had moved his arm away from beneath her lowered head and clutching hands. Now she felt her chin being raised firmly and something hard being pressed against her lips. She expected brandy, but it was only lukewarm tea from a Thermos, tasting of the plastic cup. By jerking her head, she managed to spill it, and while her kind Samaritan was mopping her up with his handkerchief, she risked a glance at her watch. Oh, Lord! Only three minutes gone.

The cup was filled again, and this time she drank, slowly, her eyes lowered.

"Good, good," he said, taking the empty cup from

her. "Now you are feeling better, my friend. You can tell me your trouble, I think."

"It's—it's little Tessie," she mumbled between sniffs. "I think she's hurt bad. She won't answer me. She's just lying there, and—and I'm frightened!"

"Where is she?"

"Over there," Belle said, waving her arm vaguely ahead. "She fell into the ditch, and now . . . she won't *move!*"

It took them several minutes to search the ditch at the side of the road, going backward and forward, stinging their hands on nettles, parting the brambles to reveal nothing but mud and rusty tins and dirty bits of paper.

"Perhaps she crawled farther up," she suggested, but the driver was now looking at her doubtfully, his sympathy turned to suspicion.

"You will wait here, please," he said, and went quickly back to his truck, glancing sharply from side to side at the high concealing hedges, the small copse on the other side of the road.

Belle ran after him. "Please don't go! Please help me," she cried.

He took no notice but walked right around his truck, kicking his tires, inspecting the lock at the back. Though by nature a friendly man, he had had to learn distrust the hard way, walking back through the cold gray streets of a new hometown, in a new country, listening for the rush of sneakered feet behind him, looking for the corner that might hide the mindless pack of thugs, waiting . . .

When he had satisfied himself that he had not been robbed, he came back to Belle.

"I think you are not truthful," he said, his dark eyes moist with reproach.

"I am!"

"I have noticed, you look over your shoulder and at your watch, and your eyes do not look like they are crying. Who is it you expect? If it is to steal, tell your friends to keep away, please, or they will be regretting it."

"I'm not a thief!" Belle said.

From the concealed entrance to the lane behind them, came the sound of an owl hooting, three times, hoo, hoo, hoo. An untimely sound in broad daylight.

"Look! There's Tessie!" Belle cried loudly, pointing in the opposite direction. "There she is."

"Where? I can see no one."

"Over there! In that field, d'you see her now? She's limping! She's hurt! Now she's fallen over!"

Behind the truck driver's back, unnoticed, a freckled boy led out a huge gray shape, a vast wrinkled shadow that moved with swaying grace across the road and into the small wood. Its enormous feet made no sound on the asphalt. Once in the wood, dead leaves muffled its tread, the small branches parting to make way for its bulk, rustled quietly as if in the wind.

And then the fat lump had to tread on a dead stick! There was a crack like a pistol shot, and the driver swung around. He stared. Then he grasped Belle by the arm and marched her across the road.

It was not a big wood. Defying the laws of perspective, it seemed to grow smaller as they approached it; the trees moving farther apart, holes appearing in the thick green. Belle could see, quite plainly, slices of Tessie between the trees, like a jigsaw coming apart. She glanced sideways at her companion. Perhaps he would mistake that creased gray leg for a tree trunk, that gently swinging tail for a broken branch in the wind. . . .

"There is an elephant in that wood," he said.

"Oh, sure," she said, laughing falsely. "And I've got a tiger in my pocket. Want to see? Look out, there's a giraffe just behind you."

"You are not fooling me," he said. He smiled happily. "It is a cow elephant, from India or Ceylon, perhaps. Not Africa, though she is very big. I know elephants, you see, so you cannot be fooling me. We had elephants at home when I was a small boy." For a moment his dark eyes looked wistful; then he turned to Belle. "Come, we will go to her, and you will tell me what naughty things you are up to, please."

Belle felt her eyes sting. She'd messed it up. She'd failed. Since the accident, nothing went right for her. *Nothing!* It was no use trying anymore.

But the long years of training took over. She was circus. Artistes didn't snivel and give up when things went wrong. Remember what Mr. Schneider was always saying—

To the driver's absolute amazement, the girl beside suddenly did three high, leaping somersaults, one af-

Vivien Alcock

ter another, held her skinny arms up in the air, and smiled at him brilliantly.

"Tara boom!" she said. "Meet Christabel, of Cosmo and Christabel, the Star Spinners. Come and see Tremendous Tessie, the largest and most lovable Indian Elephant in the world. All at Peachem's Circus next week. Tickets, three pounds, two pounds, or one pound, cheap at the price." A car horn, like a trumpet, blared loudly behind them, and she added earnestly, "Best move your truck, mister. It's blocking the road."

12

The problem of kidnapping an elephant is its sheer size. Its color is modest; a patchy gray merging into the leafy shadows, matching the asphalt of the roads, blending with the gray stone of the houses, but its size lets it down. Even a small elephant is large, and they go on growing all through their lives, unlike other animals, which know when to stop. Tessie was both old and enormous.

Charlie, standing behind a tree in the inadequate wood, had heard the driver say, "There is an elephant in that wood."

His heart had jerked between dismay and relief. It was not his fault. Belle could not blame *him,* even though it was what he had secretly wanted, to be caught before they had gone too far. And yet . . . poor Tessie.

He peered around the tree. Through the shifting

curtain of leaves, he could see patches of Belle and the driver; now the pink of Belle's shirt, now a striped sleeve, rolled up to the elbow of a brown arm.

Ought he to go on? In front of him there were glimpses of grass through the trees. Something black and white—part of a cow. An invisible dog barked, a small dog by the sound of its shrill yapping—that might mean the owner close behind. He hesitated. "Wait for me in the wood," Belle had commanded. He shrugged and waited.

Belle was now doing a circus spiel. Why on earth . . . ? he thought, puzzled. Unless she was trying to charm the driver, as she had once charmed audiences in the days when she still had a pretty face and all the impudence in the world. She sounded nervous, he thought critically, no longer certain of her power to please. For some reason it made him cross to hear her fawning, like one of Madame Nanette's poodles. At any moment she'd be sitting up and begging.

Then the voices were drowned out. Tessie, mistaking the leaves that tickled her rump for flies, broke a branch off the nearest tree and began swatting her flanks with it enthusiastically. Noisily. When it caught in other branches, she ripped them off, too, until the little wood shook and tossed and crackled around them.

Charlie was too busy dodging the whipping twigs to think what to do. Besides, he doubted if he could quiet her. There was a mischievous look in the elephant's round brown eyes, as though she felt she had been standing in the wings too long and was determined to reveal herself to the audience, even if it meant uprooting every tree.

"Charlie! Stop her, you fool! The whole wood's twitching like it's got fleas."

It was Belle running up, her face flushed and excited.

"You stop her if you think it's so easy," he said furiously.

There was no need. Tessie, on hearing Belle's voice, had dropped the branch she was holding and was now standing still, trying to look innocent.

"You've just got to be firm," Belle said. "It ain't difficult."

She and the elephant both looked smug: it infuriated Charlie. He had to bite his lip to prevent himself from saying the unforgivable words that crowded his tongue: Think yourself clever, don't you? But it's *me* Mr. Schneider chose, not you—and now you're going to mess it up for me.

He did not say these words, but they remained in his mind like poison.

Belle was too full of herself to notice his mood. She was telling him about the truck driver.

"I couldn't think what to do. So I did a bit of an act, and it worked, Charlie! He said, 'Oh, you're from a circus,' as if that explained everything, as if he thought all circus people were mad, anyway. Then he laughed and went back to his truck. I think he liked me," she added with a kind of humble wonder that almost softened Charlie's heart. Then he saw that her hair was loose on her shoulders again, with a few strands falling across her scarred cheek. She was cheating already.

Noticing his glance, she pushed her hair back from her face and said quickly, untruthfully, "The shoelace must've fallen off."

He looked at her in disbelief.

"Anyway, I always used to wear it like this. I only tied it back for practice, don't you remember?"

He said nothing.

"Charlie? Can't I wear it like this, Charlie? If I don't pull it forward?"

"Oh, suit yourself," he said, feeling mean and cross. "You always do."

There was a short silence. Then she said in a subdued voice, "Well, we'd best get on, hadn't we?"

They had two fields to cross before they reached the derelict barn where they planned to shelter until it was dark. Two large, flat, exposed areas of grass with nothing taller than a thistle to hide behind. "We've got to take a few risks," Belle had said.

Charlie climbed the gate between the two fields and looked around. No farmer, no dog walkers, no children picnicking, just his luck! Nothing but a few cows, all staring at him as if trying to memorize his face in case anyone made inquiries later. Such as the police.

From here, Belle and Tessie were invisible in the wood. He waved his arm slowly from side to side, giving the signal. All clear.

They came out fast. Belle had to run to keep up with Tessie, whose lumbering, swaying walk covered the ground at an amazing speed. There was nothing comic in the sight, however, as there is when a fat woman scampers for a bus or a hippopotamus teeters down a muddy bank on its too-small feet. The elephant looked hugely impressive as she charged across the grass, her ears standing out like maps of India and her trunk rolled up. The cows stared in amazement and backed away. A bird rose shrieking into the sky. And Charlie climbed down to put the gate between them, hoping Tessie would know when to stop.

She gave up long before she reached him, looking around at Belle as if to say, "What's all the hurry about?" Then, taking hold of a clump of grass with her trunk, she sliced it off neatly at the roots with her toenails, beat it against her front leg to get rid of any earth, and stuffed it into her mouth. She obviously felt she had had enough exercise for the day.

Any minute someone might come, Charlie thought. Any minute a voice might shout, "What the devil are you doing with that elephant in my field?"

But no one came. They reached the barn undetected. Their luggage was still where they left it, behind a rusting bulk of farm machinery, long abandoned. Sacks of straw and greens and fruit for Tessie, tins of baked beans and tuna fish for themselves, ground cloths, torches, sleeping bags, and a bucket, bought secretly in nearby villages and smuggled into the barn, had all been packed away in the huge pockets Belle had sewn on either side of Tessie's crimson-and-gold saddlecloth. They had found this still in the old tin trunk in the elephant shed. Either Mrs.

O'Hara had not known it was there or she had deliberately left it behind.

Belle tethered Tessie in the darkest corner, by the tub of water they had filled before breakfast. Then she came and sat down beside Charlie. He glanced at her and away again. She looked so pleased with herself. So smug. "We've done it, Charlie!" she whispered. "We've done it!"

"So far," he said coldly.

There was a short silence. Then she shrugged and unpacked the sandwiches she had prepared. The bread was stale. The lettuce was limp and rusty-looking. He picked the cheese out and pointedly threw the rest back into the paper bag.

"It's the heat," she said apologetically. "They've gone off a bit. But there's biscuits and cake."

Another silence.

"How did things go at the farm?" she said at last, showing a polite interest, as if she thought he was sulking because he wanted praise.

He was, in fact, rather proud of the way he'd managed. The goat had been a splendid touch. Good timing and good luck, that's what Mr. Schneider always said an artiste needed. . . . At the thought of Mr. Schneider he lost any desire to boast.

"Oh, all right," he said shortly.

He knew he was behaving badly. He'd agreed to her silly plan and he ought to put a good face on it. It was mean to take it out on her because he was worried about the police and the headlines and Mr. Schneider getting to hear about it. If only she'd have

the sense to keep quiet and give him a chance to re-
cover his temper. But she hadn't.

"Why are you so cross?" she asked. "What's the
matter?"

"Nothing."

"I hate people who say 'nothing' when they've got
prickles sticking out a mile. You've been in a foul
mood ever since we met in the wood. Did you think I
didn't notice? I'm not thick, Charlie!"

"Aren't you?"

"I'll hit you in a minute!" she said furiously. "Why
are you being like this? D'you want to back out? Are
you afraid of being caught, is that it? What if we are?
They won't send us to prison, not kids of our age.
We've got nothing to lose."

That did it. "You haven't anything to lose!" he
shouted. "You don't think of anyone else, do you?
You don't care if I lose my chance—"

He broke off, furious with himself and with her.

"I don't want to talk anymore," he said. "I'm going
to sleep. I've been up half the night, lugging those
bleeding sacks, and I'm flat out. You'd better do the
same. Did you pack the alarm clock?"

"Yes."

"Best set it for eleven, then."

He lay down and turned his back on her, ready to
refuse to listen to her apologies and excuses. But she
did not say anything. Angrily, without meaning to, he
fell asleep.

When he woke up, it was dark in the barn, but he knew at once that he was alone. As he sat up something rolled to the floor. He had to feel around to find it. It was a flashlight. He switched it on, and its light confirmed what he had already sensed. Belle and Tessie had gone. The tub stood in the corner with half an inch of dirty water in the bottom. His tote bag was standing beside it, with a note pinned to it. He unfastened it and read:

Dear Charlie,
 I am sorry. I never thort. I am a pig. Tell them it was all me. Tell them you did not know nothing about it and been looking for me. That way you will not get into trouble.

love, Belle

P.S. Please do not tell where I am going.

He ran out of the barn into the cool dusk and gazed around. The fields were empty. Even the cows had vanished.

"Belle!" he called wildly, running toward the wood. "Belle, where are you? Wait for me! *Please!*"

Where had she gone? It was only twilight. She wouldn't have started her journey yet. She must be hiding somewhere.

"Belle! Belle!"

No answer.

It was darker in the wood, and he crashed and stumbled around, scraping his elbows and knees. She was not there. Crying now, he ran along the verge of the Summaton road, passing the white gate with the for-sale sign beside it. The house itself was invisible behind tall fir trees. He did not know it was empty and never even glanced at it. Belle, hiding with Tessie behind the trees, heard him go by.

13

It was midnight now. Belle stood by the gate of the empty house and watched the few late cars go by, yellow-eyed as tigers in the night. She could see their headlights flickering through the hedges long before they came into sight. It was time to go.

If only she wasn't so tired! Her arms and legs ached. For ages, while Charlie slept, she had struggled in the barn, trying to drag the loaded saddlecloth onto the back of the kneeling elephant. It was too heavy for her. Hopeless. Then Tessie had taken over. Air whooshing up her trunk in great, hopeful sniffs, the elephant had begun to unpack the pockets.

A tin of baked beans hit Belle on the knee. Apples rolled across the dirty floor of the barn and lost themselves in dark corners. A tube of toothpaste was trodden on and split, whitening the great toes like mint-fresh frostbite. The elephant was enjoying herself.

It was the right idea. Unpack everything, fasten on the empty saddlecloth, put everything back. Easy. Or would have been, had not Tessie thought it was a game, throwing things out almost as fast as Belle could bundle them in, sneaking tomorrow's carrots into her mouth, tossing hay over her shoulder.

And still Charlie slept on.

Part of Belle was mean enough to want to prod him with her toe, as if by accident. To beg, "Please come with me. I can't manage without you."

She had never been alone. She had been born with the noise of the circus in her ears; shouts and laughter, whistling and hammering, dogs barking and the band playing. Now it was all gone, her mom and dad were gone, and that was bad enough. But parting with Charlie was the worst thing of all.

Still, it had to be done. He had saved her life: she could hardly repay him by spoiling his.

Good luck. See you sometime, she thought.

The old circus adieu. On a par with "chin up and keep smiling," "the show must go on," and all the other stuff that had been pumped into her ears since she was a baby. Oddly enough, it helped her now.

To an invisible audience, to the sound of her heart drumming, she led the elephant out on parade; across the two fields, around the copse, and into the garden of the empty house by the back gate. She had had to trust to luck, for it was all she had left. It did not let her down. They reached the garden unobserved and hid behind the tall firs, waiting for the night.

No one disturbed them. No exploring boy, no

weary tramp, came near them. No house agent called with a belated client. Only Charlie's footsteps, running through the gathering dark, his voice tolling dismally:

"Belle! Belle! Belle!"

She kept silent. Let him go. Let him have his chance to be a star.

This noble thought warmed her for all of two minutes. Then she was cold again, and frightened. There was no one to clap. She had always needed an audience cheering her on. Alone, she felt very small and insignificant. A nobody. A nothing.

The elephant was standing patiently by her side; like a tame volcano, shaken occasionally by tiny eruptions. She had hiccups. Been drinking from the ornamental pool, probably swallowed a goldfish . . . supposing she was sick? No good worrying now.

"Forward, Tess," Belle said. "Forward, old girl." They crossed the road and started on their long journey.

Seven miles to Yald Forest by road. How many by field and paths? Fifteen? Twenty? A hundred? At two o'clock in the moonlit morning she was lost. She sat down on the dew-wet grass and cried.

She did not know where she was. She did not know where her map was. She only knew that fields had gates in the stupidest places, had barbed wire woven into their hedges, and that no way, no way at all, could an elephant climb a stile. And the fat-faced moon was a deceiver; now flattening a pitted meadow so that she tripped and fell, now exaggerating each tiny irregularity so that she stepped too high over shadows and jarred every aching bone. It was no good.

"I can't . . . I can't . . . Somebody help me," she whimpered.

The elephant stood motionless; silent, majestic, silvered by the moon. *She* had not suffered. The huge cushioned circles of her feet had seemed to skim over the uneven ground like clouds. She had ambled forward when Belle told her to, stood still when Belle told her to; an old, patient, well-trained animal.

But every now and then she would lift her great head and sniff the night air with her trunk. Then her pace had quickened. . . . Lord knew where she thought she was going, what ancient memories called her. Or perhaps she was merely looking for a warm shed or tent to sleep in.

Belle rubbed her eyes. "What shall we do, Tess?" she asked.

As if in answer, the elephant swung her trunk toward Belle and pulled at her gently. Get up? Why? What was the point? They could be going around in circles. For all Belle knew, Goosebeak Farm might be hiding behind that clump of trees. She almost wished it were, with its warm kitchen. Where was Charlie now? she wondered. Snug in his bed, dreaming of the big top? Out searching for her with Mr. Thorpe? Well, let them find her!

Now the elephant was prodding her.

"Stop it!" she said.

What did Tessie want? She couldn't be hungry again, not after all she'd eaten. Thirsty?

"Suck the grass, then. It's wet enough."

Too wet to sleep on. A mist was creeping up, hugging the ground. Must be a river nearby. Belle got wearily to her feet.

"All right then. Drinkies."

But which way? The black hedges barred her view. Perhaps Tessie could smell the water. "Go on, then. Lead us to it."

The elephant, puzzled, did not move. Belle looked up at the thick neck, the high shoulders half-covered by the bulging saddlecloth. Good view from up there.

All the time, walking, running, stumbling beside the elephant, she had known she ought to be riding her. Urging her on, instead of holding her back. Elephants, Mr. Murphy had once told her, could walk ten miles in an hour. Or more. Even an old elephant, she thought, could probably do seven. It was not as if she had never ridden her before. Many times she had knelt on the looped trunk and allowed herself to be lifted up until she could clutch the headband and scramble onto Tessie's neck. But that was before the accident. Before she lost her nerve.

And now? Without Mr. Murphy standing by, sharp-eyed, ready to catch her if she slipped? With her knees weak and her head spinning? Supposing Tessie moved at the wrong time? Supposing she got impatient and shrugged Belle off like a fly? Trod on her in the dark!

No. She couldn't do it. She was a coward. Not circus anymore but an outsider, a "flattie." Dawn would come, and she and Tessie would be discovered cowering in this miserable field. At least, Belle would be cowering, sniveling, waiting to be taken back in disgrace. Not Tessie. Gentle, patient, loving animal, she would be standing there, guarding her young friend. They would take her away—how many tins of cat's meat would she make?

Four o'clock in the morning. Charlie got to his feet, yawning and stretching. Behind him, in the whispering, breathing, rustling darkness of the enclosed forest, something squealed. It was a pitiful, shivering sound. Hide, little creature, run back to your hole before the owl gets you, he thought. It must have been an animal. Couldn't possibly be Belle. But he could not rid himself of the feeling that, somewhere, she, too, was lost and frightened.

It was impossible that she could have gotten here before him. A truck had given him a lift almost immediately, and he had been waiting ever since. For hours and hours, sitting on the ground with his back resting against the closed gate, he had stared from the shadows to the silvery road; at first hopefully, then anxiously, and now with the dull certainty that she would never come.

Had she changed her plan, not trusting him, and entered the forest another way? Or had she been caught already? Soon it would be dawn. Early risers would be waking. Milk trucks would go rattling over the cattle grid on the road. It would be too late.

If I shut my eyes and count to a hundred, let her be there when I open them again. . . . But there were too many noises in the night for him to take the chance. Though he was guarding the gate to the bridle path, the road itself was protected only by a cattle grid. This kept the wild ponies and donkeys and deer safe in the forest, but would it keep out an elephant? Tessie's huge feet could easily span the rungs, padded feet that might not even rattle the metal bars as she stole past him while he sat with his eyes shut like an idiot. He dared not risk it.

So he went on staring up the empty road, jerking up his heavy eyelids every time he felt them falling. Now he seemed to see a grotesque shadow swaying silently up the grass verge. He looked at it sourly. He had been deceived before by windblown shadows, and this one was not even the right shape. Besides, there was no one walking beside the shadow. No one sitting on its neck. It was just another damn trick of the moonlight. Any moment it would dissolve into a thousand tossing leaves. . . .

But the shadow kept on advancing, getting larger and more oddly shaped by the moment, a monster growing out of the night. Three huge heads it had, and a single dim yellow eye. . . . Then it stepped into a pool of moonlight and turned into Tessie, her figure distorted by the bulging pockets on her saddlecloth and a bicycle lamp tied to her headband, the battery almost flat.

But where was Belle? What had happened?

He ran forward, shouting:

"Where is she? What have you done with her? I'll kill you if you've hurt her!"

"Charlie!"

Now he saw Belle. She was not so much riding the elephant as glued to it, close as wallpaper. Her cheek was resting against the leathery skin, her hands clinging to the headband and her feet thrust into the pockets among the apples and hay. She looked so strange lying there, a creature of moonlight, her eyes enormous in her silvery face, her hair spreading out like pale water over the elephant's massive head, and for a moment he could only stare at her as if she were a stranger from another world.

Then she giggled, and the spell was broken.

"Where the devil have you been?" he demanded.

"Everywhere."

"I've been waiting here all night."

"I got lost."

"You had the map—"

"Couldn't find it."

"You're hopeless, aren't you? Useless. Just as well I came."

She smiled down at him and said cockily, "I thought I might find you waiting here. Hogging my big act." Then she said sharply, *"Car coming!"*

Charlie opened the gate to the bridle path and let them through. The three of them walked silently into the dark forest and vanished among the trees.

14

Black leaves blotted out the moon. The fading lamp on Tessie's headband, like a visible echo, lit their way briefly. Then it went out. Unperturbed, the elephant walked on.

"Stop!" Belle cried.

Too late. Twigs combed her hair spitefully and raked her shoulders. She flung her arms up in front of her face, and something hit her shoulder, pushing her off-balance. A handful of leaves came away in her fingers. She was slipping, falling . . . the high wire, the circus ring far below her . . .

"Charlie!" she screamed.

It was not sawdust but a prickly bush that received her, breaking her fall and preserving her bones. Her nerve, however, the little remnant she'd had left, was shattered. She began to whimper.

A man's voice called out of the dark, "Hello? Who's there?"

She stuffed her knuckles into her mouth and was silent. The smell of elephant was strong in her nose. She felt it must be spreading through the trees, a give-away, a nasal advertisement, sharp as a circus trumpet.

A second voice mumbled sleepily, and the man said in reply, "Something woke me. A scream, I think. Then I heard someone crying."

"Oh, hell, the boys . . ."

"A nightmare, I expect. I'll go and see."

Splinters of light pricked the darkness. On Belle's left, leaves lit to a brilliant emerald. Then something blue . . . tents! There were tents among the trees!

A hand touched hers, and she jumped. Charlie's voice breathed in her ear, "Come on. I've got Tess."

They edged away from the light, arms outstretched to fend off the invisible trees. Dead twigs cracked beneath their feet.

The man said sharply, "There's something moving over there!"

The light, broken up by the dark trees into a hundred golden arrows, was turning toward them. . . .

"What's up?" It was a boy's voice now, young and shrill. "Sir? Is that you, sir? What's happening?"

Belle whinnied loudly.

"A pony," the man said, and laughed. "Only one of the forest ponies. Go back to sleep."

The light turned away before it reached them. In

the shadows Belle felt Charlie pat her on the back, and she glowed with pleasure.

More boys' voices now.

"Sir, I want to go home. I don't like it here."

"What's that horrible smell?"

"It's Roger. Sir, I want to change my tent. Roger stinks."

"I don't! Anyway, you snore. Sir, he's been keeping me awake."

Belle and Charlie crept away, leaving the voices behind them. They blundered deeper into the forest, which resisted them, scratching their faces and entangling their feet.

"Charlie," Belle whispered, pulling her hair out of something prickly. "Didn't you bring your flashlight?"

"They'd see the light. Best go on a bit."

"It's so dark."

"Feel your way."

They went on and on. Unseen leaves slapped them, twigs poked them, branches brushed aside by the elephant whipped back in their faces. Now, not a yard away, an invisible creature sprang to its feet and crashed through the undergrowth.

Startled, the elephant raised her trunk and trumpeted into the night.

Birds exploded from the leaves above their heads. Small animals scuttled away in terror. Belle felt Tessie move. She grabbed for her ear and missed. The warm soft-crinkled skin—a leg, a stomach, another leg—brushed past her hands, and the elephant was gone.

"Stop! Tessie, stop!"

She had a horrible vision of another camp, of a vast foot descending on a tent, of a small boy oozing between the great toes like jam.

There was a loud rustling, a splashing, then a steady gurgle.

Charlie switched on his flashlight. Tree trunks sprang out all around them, like great stone columns, greenish-gray in the light. Trees, bushes, ferns . . . no elephant.

"Tessie!" Belle yelled in panic. "Tessie!"

A spray of water hit her face. She grabbed the flashlight from Charlie and shone it straight into a mischievous round eye, peering at her through a small gap in some thick holly. Getting down on her hands and knees, she wriggled beneath the low branches. She could hear Charlie following her, cursing under his breath.

The elephant was standing in a stream, cut deep in the floor of the forest. One of the high banks had crumbled, forming a small beach, half mud, half stones, and now heavily printed with elephant tracks.

It was much lighter. They were in a small clearing. On all sides huge trees pushed through the undergrowth, elbowing each other for room. Here and there they tilted at mad angles, dead and unable to lie down. Bushes filled the spaces between them and overhung the stream, so that it seemed to come from nowhere, swirl around the elephant's legs, and vanish again. Fallen branches spanned the hidden water or lay piled together, as if for a bonfire, with ferns lick-

ing through them like green flames. High above their
heads a pale patch of sky shone through the leaves.

"It's almost day," Charlie whispered. "Listen, the
birds are singing."

"I'm so tired."

"Shall we stay here? Seems safe enough. What
d'you think?"

"Dunno."

Belle sat down on the bank, half asleep, barely conscious of Charlie leading the elephant out of the
stream. In the dim light the water looked discolored,
reddish from the iron in the ground.

"Oh, go to bed!" Charlie said kindly, throwing her
sleeping bag at her. "You look half dead. I'll see to
Tessie."

"I must tether her . . ."

"I'll do it."

"But . . ."

"Don't fuss. I can manage."

She was too tired to argue. In her sleeping bag in a
nest of ferns, she was falling, falling—only to wake
with a jerk, seeming to hear her father's voice in her
ears. "Always check everything. Don't take risks.
Life is dangerous enough." Her mind was full of ter-
rors; the dark forest, the sleeping boys, the great animal standing in a stream of blood. . . . She struggled against sleep—wasn't there something she
should have done? Told Charlie? What was it? The
rope, use the rope . . . it was no good. Her eyes
closed again.

On the other side of the clearing the elephant

shifted her feet. She walked forward, felt the jerk of the tether on her hind leg, and swung her head around to look at it. Backing a little, she turned and pulled at the chain with her trunk. The stake to which it was attached slid gently out of the soft ground.

15

Someone was shaking Charlie and shouting his name. Go away. It can't be time to get up yet. Go away.

"Wake up! Charlie, *wake up!*"

He opened his eyes and saw Belle's face, freckled with sunlight and shadows. Her mouth was quivering.

"Tessie's gone," she said.

"What?"

"She's gone."

"She can't have gone," he said stupidly.

She turned from him impatiently and started running backward and forward in the clearing, calling, "Tess! Tess!" her voice as high as a bird's.

There was confusion everywhere. Clothes and cabbage leaves, tins and flashlight batteries were scattered over the ground. Wisps of hay decorated the bushes like bleached tinsel. Belle's blue T-shirt floated in the stream.

"What happened?" he asked fearfully. "Has she gone crazy?"

"No, of course not. She just likes unpacking. And she's been at the food. Ain't got no table manners." Belle's smile was shaky, but at least she had attempted a joke. Hadn't shouted at him, though it was his fault. *He* had tethered Tessie. "Leave it to me," he'd said. Feeling guilty and miserable, he mumbled, "She can't have gone far." Another stupid remark, which Belle ignored. He didn't blame her. Tessie'd had all the time they had slept. She could be anywhere.

"Tessie! Tessie!" Now Belle was parting the branches on this side and that, trying to see through the crowding leaves.

Charlie scrambled to his feet, tripped over a hairbrush, trod on the recorder Uncle Bert had given him for Christmas. Automatically he picked it up. It seemed to be undamaged.

"I dunno where to start looking," Belle said helplessly, and turned.

She caught sight of the recorder in his hands. Lost her temper. "That's right! Don't worry about Tessie! Don't help me! Just stand there and play us a tune—" She broke off. Her eyes widened and she said, "Oh, Charlie, you're *clever!* That'll fetch her. Go on!"

He looked at her, pleased but bewildered by her sudden admiration, not liking to admit he had no idea what had caused it.

"Go on," she said again; then, anxiously, "Don't say you've forgotten how it goes?"

What goes? Oh, of course! He put the recorder to his lips. Loud as he could, his cheeks blowing out like freckled balloons, he began to play the music for the entrance of the elephants.

There was a rustling of leaves, coming nearer, getting louder, a crackling of twigs, and the bushes parted.

But it was a man who walked into the clearing. He was tall, thin, and somewhat untidy. Bits of bracken stuck to his crumpled trousers, a buttonless thread hung from his shirt, and he wore a lopsided haversack on his back. His fair, faded hair grew in long wisps all over his head and chin: he looked as if he needed mowing.

He smiled into their disappointed faces and said, "Hello. I thought you were Pan."

"No," Charlie muttered. "Sorry."

"We ain't seen no one around here," Belle said. "Have we, Charlie?"

"No."

"*Pan,*" the man repeated. "You know, the merry, merry pipes of Pan."

They stared at him. He smiled back at them so amiably that Charlie found himself apologizing. "Sorry. It was only me playing my recorder."

The man tilted back his head and laughed.

Behind his back, making surprisingly little noise, the elephant loomed out of the bushes. The huge creature stood among the little shaking leaves and gazed around. She seemed puzzled, so unusual a circus ring. And so small an audience. The man was still laughing. Hadn't heard her come. Had no idea she was standing behind him, like a house. Her eyes fixed with interest on his haversack.

She took a step toward him. . . .

"*Stop!*" Belle shouted.

At one and the same time, the elephant stood still, and the man stopped laughing. It was uncanny.

"I'm sorry. It was rude of me to laugh," the man said. "Unforgivable. Why should you have heard of Pan? Why in the world? No reason. I am a fool. *Mea culpa.*"

Behind his back the elephant stretched out a hopeful trunk toward his haversack.

"Sit down!" Belle cried.

Tessie sat obediently. The man looked surprised, then came forward and sat down, too, on a log.

"Thank you," he said.

There was a pause. The man just sat there, smiling, as if he thought they were going to offer him tea. Except that his nose kept wrinkling, he seemed quite unaware of the elephant sitting behind him.

Probably thinks it's us stinking, and is too polite to mention it, thought Charlie. Come to that, I expect we do, a bit. Slept in our clothes, haven't washed since yesterday morning . . .

"Are you camping here?" he asked, and began to turn his head. At any moment he'd see Tessie! Couldn't miss her, sitting there, big as a bus, twiddling her trunk.

Belle stepped quickly in the way to block his view. "I got to be excused. Don't watch! It's *rude!*"

She said this so sharply that the man went pink in the face and looked away immediately.

"My dear child, I didn't intend . . . I'd no idea . . ."

"Well, don't turn around. I hate people staring at me!" she said, and ran past him, across the clearing to Tessie.

"I assure you," the man said, looking at Charlie in bewilderment, "I had no idea of embarrassing your sister. . . ."

"Cousin," Charlie explained. "She's shy."

Behind the man's back, Belle had gotten Tessie to her feet and pushed her through the bushes. Then she held one hand up, the five fingers spread wide, before vanishing after the elephant.

Five minutes, Charlie translated. Five minutes to get rid of the man. How? Say straight out, "Go away, you old goat. We don't want you here."

But the man's face, sandwiched between his wispy hair and beard, looked so friendly. A friendly old goat; it would be like kicking an animal. While Charlie hesitated, he found he was being offered half a bar of chocolate.

"I'm afraid it's a bit sticky," the man said, carefully wrapping the remaining half in its silver paper. "I'll keep this for your cousin."

"She won't come back while you're here," Charlie said quickly. "Like I said, she's shy. Hates being looked at."

"Is it her scar?"

"Her scar's all right," Charlie said shortly. *"I* don't mind it."

"No, indeed . . . in fact, I think it makes her look rather dashing, like a girl pirate. I only meant it was a pity if it worries her," the man said gently. "It's a difficult time, being a child. . . . Was it a traffic accident?"

"No. She fell off something." Charlie said, and then, because the man looked so kind and concerned, added impulsively, "The thing is—she's lost her head for heights."

"That's very understandable."

"D'you think she'll get over it?"

"I'm afraid I've no idea. You'd have to ask a doctor. Does it matter?"

"Yes," said Charlie gloomily.

He had never dared ask anyone before. It mattered too much. He didn't quite know why—there were other jobs in the circus. Belle's own mother never got her feet off the ground. She just stood in front of a painted board while Uncle Bert outlined her plump, glittering figure with knives. And there was Mavis, the juggler's assistant, who handed him the props and then pranced around, clicking her fingers and waggling her hips in time to the music. Belle could do that. Any fool could!

But what a comedown! He remembered how she used to swing high above his head, laughing down at him. He remembered her walking the low wire, light as thistledown, calling, "Come on, Charlie! It's easy. You can do it! You can be as good as me—almost."

He was better than Belle now. He ought to be pleased, but he wasn't. He was *miserable*. What good was it going up in the world if he had to leave her behind on the sawdust, a skinny little bird with clipped wings?

The man, watching him, was puzzled. The boy looked so upset. How could it matter so much? Still, it was none of his business.

"I must be getting on," he said, rising to his feet, "or I'll be late for lunch and my wife will be cross with me. She's not fond of walking. Rings on her fingers and corns on her toes, that's my fine lady."

He had been hoping to make the boy smile, but Charlie just said dully, "Good-bye, then."

The man hesitated. Then he said, "You know, it might be worth asking a doctor. I believe there's some sort of therapy that might work. Not that I know much about it. But I saw a program on television . . . actually, it was about people who are afraid of flying."

Charlie's face brightened. In his mind he saw not airplanes but the big top, with the high flyers swooping and somersaulting above the safety net.

"Please, mister, can you tell me about it?" he asked eagerly. "I'll come with you part of the way. If you don't mind. Look, we can get through here. Careful, it's a bit prickly. Let me push back that branch. . . ."

In the forest behind them the elephant trumpeted.

"Good God, what was that?" the man said.

Charlie, startled, had let go of the branch that swung back, its twigs getting entangled with his clothes and hair. He struggled wildly to free himself.

"Here, let me help you," the man said. "You're tearing your shirt." He noticed that the boy had gone quite white beneath his freckles and added reassuringly, "It must have been one of the wild donkeys. Horrible din, wasn't it? Quite enough to startle anyone."

"Yes, a donkey," Charlie babbled gratefully. "It was a donkey." He could have laughed with relief. People only heard what they expected to hear, he realized, and who would think of an elephant in Yald Forest?

The man smiled, glad to see that the boy had recovered from his fright. They went off together, leaving the clearing empty.

16

Belle sat on the grassy bank, listening. Leaves whispered together. Water chattered with the pebbles in the stream. Birds above her head chirruped to one another. All the forest seemed to be conversing: she alone had no one to talk to. Charlie was not back.

It was over two hours since she had heard him go off with the man. Two hours in which she had tidied away their belongings and repacked them neatly in the saddlebags. The map of Yald Forest had turned up among Charlie's shirts, and she left it out on the grass beside her. Then she had made baked beans and tuna fish sandwiches, wrapped them up in plastic wrap, and waited.

And waited, growing more hungry and more anxious each minute.

"Silly fool's gotten lost," she muttered.

The elephant, tethered by a long rope to a tree, was

dreaming on her feet. She rumbled softly at the sound of Belle's voice but did not open her eyes.

"If I go off to look for him, I'll get lost, too, and then where will you be?"

The elephant did not answer.

"So what am I to do?"

The elephant had no ideas to offer. There was something very irritating about the way she stood, placidly snoozing while Belle fidgeted with worry.

"You're not much company, are you?"

The elephant opened her eyes and looked fondly and sleepily at Belle. Then she sat down and rolled over onto her side. Her great gray belly humped up from a sea of green ferns like a fissured rock. Dappled with sunlight and smudged with mud, it blended into the background, becoming part of the forest, a pattern of light and shade.

This is where she belongs, thought Belle, here in this wild nowhere. Not decked out in crimson and gold in a circus ring. Poor old Tess, she should've had a mate and calves of her own to love. Not just me and Charlie. Still, too late for that. It's us or the slaughterhouse now, old girl.

She picked up the map and spread it on the ground. Frowned. It was not an encouraging picture. Through the green hair of the forest great bald patches showed; pink for heathland and yellow for downland. Gray scurfy villages hung in a net of roads, and there were red spots everywhere, for camping, fishing, horse riding, and ancient monuments. Many of the green areas were divided up with dotted lines and labeled: Canfield Enclosure, Cresswell Lawn Enclosure, Foxleap Enclosure . . .

Charlie had warned her. "Look at it, Belle," he had said. "We'll never get through that lot unnoticed. It'll be crowded with trippers."

And she had said, with the careless optimism that had so often got her into trouble, "Oh, it'll be all right. We'll find somewhere to hide."

Well, she supposed they had found somewhere, this little clearing in a tuft of trees. But already a man had come and walked off with Charlie. And now—now she could hear voices!

She jumped to her feet and stared through the leaves. Saw nothing but trees. She glanced back at the gray hump in the ferns. Would she know it was an elephant if she didn't know it was an elephant? Difficult to tell. Best leave Tessie sleeping and go and meet trouble halfway. Head it off somehow. She parted the branches carefully and wriggled through.

A figure rose out of the leaves and grabbed hold of her, crooking an elbow around her neck.

"Hey! I got another one!" it said.

She could not see who was holding her. She kicked backward, but her soft sandals made no impression on a stout leg. The arm tightened around her neck, choking her. She could not scream.

Now her captor dragged her back into the clearing. More figures stepped out from the trees. There were four of them, strange creatures, their faces painted with mud and half hidden by the leafy twigs attached to their hats. At first she thought they were soldiers.

Then she noticed that they were wearing faded denims below their patched khaki shirts, and one was a boy, no bigger than she was, holding a homemade bow and arrow.

A tall figure, who appeared to be their leader, strutted up and looked her over. In his mud-stained face his gray eyes were as cold and pale as glass. He had a switchblade in his hands, and he pointed it at her, drawing patterns in the air as if planning how to cut her up. Then, as she stared at him in terror, he began cleaning his nails with it.

"Bring in the prisoner," he said.

Two more figures appeared, holding between them a struggling, squirming, cursing boy. It was Charlie. His face was patched with red, his lip split and bleeding, his shirt torn.

"Let her go!" he shouted. "I'll kill you!"

"Shut up," said the leader. "You keep quiet if you don't want your bird carved." He looked back at Belle, then put out his hand and pushed the hair back from her cheek. "Been done already, by the look of it. How'd you get that, eh?"

She could not speak. She could hardly breathe.

"Let go 'er neck, Jerry. You're strangling 'er. She won't scream. Will you, chick?"

The arm around her neck was taken away.

"What d'you want?" she croaked painfully. "Who are you?"

She could see now that they were not men but youths, the oldest no more than sixteen or seventeen.

"We're outlaws," said the one with the knife.

"Robin 'Ood and 'is merry men. Robbing the rich and giving to the poor. The rich, that's you. The poor, that's us."

"I ain't got no money."

"That's what 'e said." The youth jerked his thumb at Charlie. "And 'e were a dirty little liar, weren't 'e?" He patted his pocket. "Thirty-five pound 'e 'ad on 'im. Not a bad haul."

"I couldn't help it, Belle!" Charlie cried, close to tears. It was all they had left of their fund. They *needed* it.

"Turn your pockets out—Belle, is it?" the youth said. "Ding dong Belle, let's 'ear you chime. Come on, 'and it over like a good girl, or we'll 'ave to search you. Hey, what about it? Would you like that? Not ticklish, are you?"

"Leave her alone!" Charlie shouted, struggling helplessly.

But Belle had heard what none of them seemed to have noticed, a great heaving and rustling in the ferns behind her. She might not have a knife, but perhaps she had something better; a tank, a juggernaut . . .

"Don't move!" she said.

Even as she spoke, she saw the leader's jaw drop, as if a hinge had broken. The black stripes of mud now patterned a skin gone white, and from this zebra-face, his light eyes, fixed in terror, stared over her shoulder.

"She'll attack if you move!" Belle said fiercely. "She'll mash you all into the mud. For God's sake, keep still."

They stood like statues, except that they trembled.

They hardly seemed to breathe. The young boy whimpered once, then gagged his mouth with his hand. The two youths who had been holding Charlie had let go and were trying to inch back into the bushes.

"Don't move!" Belle said again, and they froze.

She looked at Charlie, trying not to laugh. To her astonishment he, too, was staring past her, his eyes wide and frightened. Puzzled, she turned around.

The elephant, risen out of the ferns, no longer looked the gentle animal they had known. Her ragged ears stood rigidly out from her head. Her trunk swung like a truncheon. She was swaying backward and forward, her furious eyes fixed on the youth who had been holding Belle. Here, in this great green, tangled world, old memories awoke. The elephant smelled fear. Her skinny little calf was frightened, and the great animal prepared to defend her. Raising her trunk aloft, she gave the trumpet scream of battle.

But now Belle was walking toward her, making soft noises, repeating the odd sound that the elephant knew meant she must not move her feet. Opposing instincts warred in her great head.

"Stand, Tess! Stand!"

The small, clear voice penetrated the dark confusions in her mind. She shook her head as if to clear it, and dust flew from her ears. Then, suddenly, she turned and vented her fury on an innocent bush. She smashed it with her trunk, pounded it into the earth and trampled on it, plucked the broken thing up by its roots and beat it against a tree. Only when it was a mangled corpse did she toss it away and stand quietly, her sides heaving.

Belle laid a shaking hand on her trunk.

"Gently, old girl. Gently, my fat darling. Hush now. It's all right."

She stood, soothing the elephant, and heard Charlie's voice behind her, rich with satisfaction.

"Get in line, you lot," he was saying. "I'll have my money back for a start—and that knife! That's better. Anyone else got any weapons? Throw 'em down over there. You're *our* prisoners now."

Prisoners! What on earth are we going to do with them? Belle wondered. Can't hand them over to the police, we're in hiding ourselves. Tie 'em up with rope . . . Rope!

She looked down at the long tether, lying like a snake in the ferns, hidden from all eyes but her own. Would it have held? She wondered. She went on stroking the elephant, whispering, "What have we done to you, Tess? You're changing. The forest is changing you. Don't forget us. Don't forget you love me. Elephants aren't supposed to forget."

17

It was odd that after such a beginning they should become friends. Well, friends of a sort. They did not trust one another, yet they sat, talking and laughing companionably, sharing their food. Charlie was not certain how it had come about.

First they had been his enemies, then his prisoners . . . perhaps that was the trouble. What can you do with prisoners if you don't have a handy jail to put them in? No chance of shutting the door and forgetting them. There they were, six big sullen louts and a sniveling boy. So you start talking—well, you can't just stand staring at each other in silence, and the next thing you know you're swapping stories. . . .

It began when the boy had started coughing, a dry, rapid cough that shook his shoulders and made him gasp for breath.

"Pat him on the back, can't you?" Charlie said,

thinking he was choking. Then he saw, out of the corner of his eye, the leader slip his hand quickly into a pocket. "Hey! Stop that!" he said sharply.

"Don't worry, kid. It ain't a gun," the leader said, bringing out a crumpled paper bag and holding it up. Somebody sniggered. "Fruit drops, see? For Billy. 'E don't like cough sweets. You ain't got no objections to 'im 'aving one, I 'ope."

"No."

" 'E's got a bit of a cold," the leader explained, unwrapping a sweet and handing it to the coughing boy with an air of concern that seemed odd from such a sharp, dangerous-looking youth. He then held the bag out to Charlie.

"Like one?"

Charlie hesitated.

"They ain't poisoned, cross me 'eart," the leader said, rather mockingly.

"All right, then. Thanks."

It was as if he had accepted an olive branch. Immediately the outlaws relaxed.

" 'Ave a cigarette?" one of them offered.

"Mind if we sit down?" another said. "Me legs still 'urts. You didn't 'alf kick 'ard."

"Yeh, you put up a good fight," the leader said admiringly. " 'Ave to 'and it to you. Proper little scrapper, you are."

" 'E may be a featherweight, but 'e ain't chicken," said a black youth, on whose ebony skin the mud smears looked sallow.

They all laughed at this. "You can say that again, Pete. 'E sure ain't chicken."

Charlie could not help being pleased, even though he guessed that they were deliberately flattering him. Behind his back he could hear Belle still talking softly to the elephant and was glad she could not see the silly smirk on his face.

"What's your name, kid?" the leader asked.

"Charlie."

"I'm Flick, and Billy 'ere's me kid brother. Them's . . ." He waved his hand at the others and gabbled a list of names so quickly that it sounded like one word, "Jobertdavejerripete."

Dazed by the excitements of the day, Charlie made no attempt to distinguish between them. It seemed right that the ring of faces, disguised with mud and shadowed by the leafy fronds on their hats, should have only one name. They were like a many-headed creature, a dragon of the forest, friendly now, but never quite to be trusted. Even when he got to know them better, something of this impression of them as a combined personality remained. He often could not tell who was speaking.

Now he smiled at them uncertainly and said, "What am I going to do with you?"

They looked at him reproachfully, saying, "Why, we're friends now, ain't we?"

That's how it had begun. Now, hours later, he and Belle were sitting outside the outlaws' hideout, drinking hot tea from enamel mugs while the sun sank below the treetops and the forest closed in around them, dim, secret, and safe.

Charlie still thought of them as the outlaws, though when he had asked them what they called themselves, they had said they didn't call themselves anything.

"We ain't a kid's gang," Flick said. "We're dropouts. We don't want no part of their stinking civilization. What's it ever done for us?"

The circus children did not know. They weren't even sure what civilization was supposed to do for you. All the outlaws spoke of their world bitterly, as if it had cheated them of something. As if it would cheat anyone, given half a chance. Belle and Charlie exchanged uneasy glances: this was the world they were about to enter. No longer would the big top, with its brightly striped canvas and sparkling lights, protect them from harsh winds. They felt young and ignorant.

"You mean, you've run away from home, then?" Belle asked.

" 'Ome? What's that?" Flick asked sourly. " 'Aven't been in a 'ome since I was fifteen. Then our mum took me back. Not Billy, 'e was too young to be useful. She only wanted me. Thought I was going to get a job and support 'er. What a laugh! I emptied 'er purse one afternoon, fetched Billy out of the dump, and came out 'ere. The forest is all right. We like it 'ere."

"Won't they be looking for you?" Charlie asked.

"The police? Yeh. Bound to be. But not 'ere. Laid a false trail, didn't we?" Flick said. "I left a note for our

mum, saying as 'ow we was going to Lunnon and not
to bother coming looking for us."

"You gotta throw 'em off the scent," said the black
youth, whose name was Pete. "We was in the same
'ome, me and Bill and Jo. So when we was ready to go
off, I looked around for the biggest blabbermouth and
told 'im we was off up to the smoke. 'It's a secret,
mind,' I said, knowing 'e couldn't keep 'is mouth shut
in a sandstorm. Then we buzzed off quick and come
down 'ere, where they'll never guess in an 'undred
years. Think we're too soft to live wild, but we ain't.
We're no tame cats, mewing for milk. We manage."

"Yeh," the others agreed. "We manage all right."

They seemed to have known each other for a long
time, met in various homes, remand centers, shared
the same probation officer. Only Jerry, the one who
had grabbed Belle, had no story to offer. He was a
heavy, lumpish youth, big as a man, with a face like a
dirty pudding, and small black-currant eyes. He said
very little and smiled less. Occasionally Flick would
glance at him, and Charlie thought his expression was
uneasy.

The outlaws had lived in the forest for over three
months, right under the noses of the forest authori-
ties, and never once had been caught. Nor even seen,
unless they chose to be.

"We know our way around," they boasted. "It's
easy, if you know 'ow. We can crawl past a keeper so
close 'e could touch us with 'is 'and, only 'e don't
know we're there. We can snitch a purse out of a
picnic basket so quiet it don't disturb the flies. Oh,

there ain't a fox can outsmart us! And we got our earths, too. What d'you think of our 'ideout, eh? Not bad, is it? We 'ave them all over the forest."

Belle and Charlie had been shown over the hideout and had been impressed. Even close by, it was impossible to tell it was there. It looked like a bush, a living bush with green leaves. Only when you'd gone around the back and crawled under the low branches of a rhododendron could you see that the bush was trained over a trapdoor. This trapdoor itself was stuck all over with dried grass and needed sharp eyes to discover it. Underneath, the ground had been hollowed out to make a low, small room, boarded with planks of wood and roofed with old tarpaulins ("It's shocking 'ow careless people are with their property"). They had a primus stove and a kettle and an old black frying pan. Their beds were of dried bracken with a few gray blankets. Too few, thought Charlie, and was glad their sleeping bags were packed away from envious eyes. Still, it must have been hot in there with all seven of them. Like a sardine can. He wouldn't fancy it himself. But you couldn't deny that it was clever.

"You can't stay here forever, though," Belle said. "I mean, when winter comes . . ."

It was as if she had said a dirty word, stubbed out a cigarette on a child's balloon. There was a shocked silence while they glared at her.

Then Flick said curtly, "We'll manage. Some'ow."

Belle looked doubtful, and Charlie was afraid she would argue and turn the outlaws against her. Since she had walked fearlessly up to the rampaging elephant, they had treated her with respect. She was their young queen, a right good 'un, a brave little chick. Belle had glowed under their open admiration, laughing and tossing back her hair, no longer ashamed of the scar that seemed, in this fierce company, like a badge of honor.

Well, she *had* been brave, though not quite as brave as they thought. And she'd been cunning, too, saying innocently, "I suppose I'd better tie her up now. Where's that rope gone?"—pretending to search in the ferns for a tether that (Charlie guessed) was already firmly attached to the elephant's ankle.

"It's an old rope," she had warned them untruthfully. "Frayed. If she gets mad, it won't hold her, no more than a cobweb would. So don't get any ideas."

No, they wouldn't, they had promised, looking uneasily at the elephant.

" 'Ow did you come by 'er, Miss?" Billy had asked. "Is she yours?"

To Charlie's surprise Belle had told them the truth, though not all of it. She had left out all names, except for their own, and did not say where they planned to end up. The outlaws' faces softened as they listened. One or two of them had murmured, "Poor old elephant. What a shame. 'Ope you make it all right."

Only Jerry had scowled and muttered that he'd prefer cans of cat food to that shoving monster any day.

Even now he kept looking resentfully across the new clearing to where Tessie was tethered.

"Do we 'ave to 'ave that stinking creature so near? Turns my stomach."

"You don't smell so sweet yourself."

"It ain't right to keep a dangerous animal."

"Tessie's not dangerous. She's as gentle as a lamb," Belle said, then added cautiously, "unless she's provoked."

"Some lamb!" Flick said, smiling at her.

"Honest! She's an old softie. Come and stroke her."

Flick was taken aback. He looked suddenly uncertain, like a boy confronted with a dare he wanted to refuse but could not. The other outlaws turned their mud-stained faces and stared silently at their leader, waiting. Jerry gave a grunting laugh and sneered.

"Go on, Flick. Flick ain't scared, is 'e? Not our leader! Not Flick the Knife."

Without meaning to, Belle had nudged the balance of power and set it rocking. No leader of a pack could afford to show cowardice. Ordeal by elephant, thought Charlie, biting back a laugh.

Yet somehow, in the leafy half-light, with the forest stirring around them, it did not seem so ridiculous. The elephant was transformed. Like the vast stone goddess of an ancient religion, she stood under the trees and watched them impassively.

At last Flick got to his feet and said, his voice strained, "Yeah. Why not?"

He and Belle walked slowly up to the elephant, who stretched out her trunk to touch Belle briefly in greeting. Then she turned her attention to Flick. Across the clearing they could hear the air whooshing through her trunk as she sniffed him all over. It made a strange sort of music, weird, primitive. He stood straight and still, like a young warrior undergoing an initiation ceremony, and the watchers held their breath. Then Flick reached up and touched the elephant's forehead, just once, before stepping back.

He laughed with relief and, turning to the others, said, "Come on, you beggars. Pay your respects to the old lady."

They went up one by one, slowly, nervously, to touch the elephant and move on. In the dim, fretted light, the figures with their mud-smeared faces and leafy hats looked like beings from a wilder planet, taking part in some dark ceremony. So strong and strange was the spell that Charlie found himself following, to touch the elephant goddess in his turn. He was shocked when Belle winked at him. It was as if a priestess had stuck her tongue out.

When he had moved on to join the others, he heard her say sternly, "No. Not you. Keep away."

It was Jerry to whom she spoke. He stood there lumpishly, just out of reach of the elephant's trunk and glowered.

"What'cher mean? Why not me?"

"She hates you. You attacked me. She'll never forget. Never forgive. Look at her."

And indeed the great animal was moving restlessly, pulling against her tether.

"Go back now," Belle said, and they scattered to the far side of the clearing.

"Is she safe?" Billy asked, his voice high and afraid. "She can't get loose, can she?"

"She'll be all right now," Belle said. "Only keep *him* away. The fat one."

Charlie glanced at Jerry and saw the black-currant eyes gleam with hate in the shadowed face. Belle had made an enemy. One who would never forget. Never forgive.

18

Somehow the outlaws had taken charge of them. "You'll never manage without us," they said. "Look 'ow easy we caught you. Babes in the wood, that's what you are. You'd end up in a campsite or a woodman's 'ut. 'Ere, let's 'ave a look at your map."

They spread it on the ground. Already the light was so poor that they had to use a flashlight. The outlaws squatted around in a tight circle, all elbows and knees, like stick insects. Only Jerry stood back, looking over their shoulders; listening, watching, not saying anything.

"We thought we'd go this way tonight," Belle said, tracing her finger over a large green area. "Hide up somewhere here for the day. Then tomorrow night we'll only have that open moor to cross."

The outlaws leaned closer so that the twigs on their hats met, forming a little forest of their own. Fingers jabbed at the map, voices excitedly warned of the dangers; a bog here, a fence there, a parking lot, men digging ditches . . . Go this way, they said, No, that way. Hide here. Hide there. Their faces, lit from below by the flashlight, looked strange, unearthly. Behind them in the twilight the tethered elephant shifted her great feet and looked down curiously at the little chattering creatures who were deciding her fate.

Finally Flick put down his finger firmly, brushing the other fingers aside. *"There,"* he said, "I'll take you there. Good spot."

Belle peered at the map.

"But it's an enclosure," she objected.

"So what? There's gates."

"Ain't they kept locked?"

"No. You can go in if you don't do no damage. It says so. No camping. No fires. Dogs to be kept on the lead." He thought for a minute. "Don't say nothing about elephants."

Belle hesitated, not liking the thought of being fenced in.

"But . . ." she began doubtfully.

It was no good. They talked her down. Everyone agreed it was the best place, a smashing place; bracken higher than your head and branches down to your knees. What about people? No trouble. They kept to the paths.

"They won't see us," Flick said. "People are dead stupid. They don't know 'ow to look."

"Kids are a nuisance, though," Pete warned them.

"Kids didn't stay on the paths."

"Sharp-eyed little beggars, some of them. You want to watch out for kids!"

"But don't worry. You leave them to us," Flick said. "We'll deal with them." Belle looked at him sharply, and he laughed. "Oh, we won't cut their throats or nothing like that. Just shove 'em around a bit. Send them back to their mums."

"Doing them a favor, really," said Pete. "Stops them getting lost. We oughta charge for it."

"We do," said Flick slyly, and they all laughed.

Belle was silent, remembering Charlie's bruised and bleeding face, the stolen money, the arm crooked around her neck. . . .

"It's a good place, honest," Flick said, mistaking the reason for her silence. "Trust us."

They had to trust them, though it became more difficult as it grew darker, and the outlaws, their camouflaged faces melting into the shadows, became whispers in the night. Belle and Charlie kept close to Tessie, comforted by her huge bulk and warm, familiar smell. Every rustle in the leaves made them jump nervously, wondering if a new friend had become an enemy again, creeping up on them in the dark. They were relieved when Flick said it was time to go.

He led them along narrow roads, keeping a scout in front and one in the rear. The forest was not fenced here.

"When they give the signal, dive for cover," he said.

"What's the signal?"

"This," Flick said, and gave a high, warbling, bird-like call. His followers vanished. One moment they were on the road and the next they were gone.

Flick laughed with pride. "See 'ow it goes?" he said. He gave the call again, and the outlaws were back, seeming to rise out of the ground.

"You ought to be a general," Charlie said admiringly as they walked on.

"Me? Fight their bloody wars for them? Risk my life for *them?* What've they ever done for me?"

He spoke so bitterly that Charlie thought he meant particular enemies, with well-known and well-hated faces.

"Who?" he asked.

"Them," Flick repeated, his voice harder than the road beneath their feet. "Everybody. Everybody who ain't one of us."

"Oh," Charlie said, then, not to be outdone, added, "We call them flatties."

"What?"

"Everyone who's not circus, that's what we call them. Flatties. We don't hate them, though." He smiled. "I mean, someone's got to pay to see us."

To his surprise Flick said impatiently, "Oh, you don't know nothing. You're just a kid," and went off to walk with Pete.

It was cold now, with a wind blowing in the trees. The road stretched in front of them, striped like a tiger in the moonlight. Twice they heard the high, warbling signal. The first time Charlie was half asleep. Taking it for a real bird, he would have gone on walking, had someone not grabbed his arm and dragged him into the trees. A car swept past, its head-lights fanning the edge of the forest, seeming to seek them out. Then it was gone.

"They only look at the road ahead," Flick said. "They don't see nothing else. People are stupid."

Charlie thought, If you were driving, it was sensible to keep your eyes on the road; but he said nothing. He could not help being impressed by Flick's efficiency. When they reached the enclosure, Pete was told to walk ahead, shining a flashlight on the path in front of the elephant. The others walked behind, stopping occasionally to scuff their feet over the gravel or brush a patch of earth with sticks.

"Try and keep 'er off the mud," Flick said, " 'er feet are too big. They'll never take that for no rabbit."

After about ten minutes Pete stopped and shone his flashlight briefly into the forest on one side. Water gleamed on the dead leaves in a wide ditch.

" 'Ere we are," he said. "Walk 'er along there. We don't want the bracken trampled. The water'll 'ide 'er tracks."

The ditch ran straight into the forest. It was darker here, and the flashlight moved so quickly, they had to hurry to keep up with it. Twice Charlie stumbled over a hidden root and fell to his knees into a wet squelch of dead leaves. He was glad when Pete led them out of the ditch and onto dry ground. A dim figure brushed past him, and Flick's voice said, "All right. This'll do."

The outlaws flopped down on the ground, disappearing into the bracken between the tall trees. Pete switched off his flashlight. From the sudden darkness a gruff voice said, "What about that stinking brute? Don't want 'er near us. It ain't safe."

There was a murmur of agreement.

Charlie said quickly, thankfully, "It's all right. We'll take her farther on. We can meet up in the morning."

"I'll come with you," Flick said. "I ain't afraid of 'er. And we don't want you getting lost, do we?"

There was no way of refusing this kind offer. Charlie put his hand in his pocket and closed his fingers around Flick's knife, glad he had not given it back. I'd best stay awake, he thought. It isn't long till dawn. It's just the dark and not knowing . . .

For some time he lay listening to the noises of the forest, the wind agitating the leaves, the sudden little scamperings in the undergrowth, an owl hooting its eternal question, Who? who?

Nearby, Flick was breathing heavily—was he really asleep? He had been nervous, worried about Tessie, insisting that they tether her a long way off, inspecting the rope and the knots with his flashlight. . . . "You sure you done it right? I don't want to be mashed up in my sleep."

Sleep. Tessie was asleep now. He could hear her snoring in the distance. It was a gentle, soothing sound, like surf on a beach, small waves stroking the shingle. When the tide was out, he and Belle danced on the sands, and the flatties loved them. They were filling his hat with silver coins, and gold. . . . Five-pound notes blew through the summer air, rustling like leaves on the trees. . . . Charlie slept.

19

Tessie had gotten free again. She was standing over the saddlebags with the tether trailing behind her, eating the last of the carrots.

"You ain't fit to look after 'er! Can't you even tie a knot proper?" It was Flick's voice that woke Belle. High and reproachful, it seemed to come from the bright sky itself.

She looked up and saw him sitting astride a branch, scowling down at her. In five other trees youths hung like pale fruit. She hardly recognized them. They had washed the mud from their faces and looked not so much clean as faded.

"I did!" she protested. "I checked it twice. You saw me do it. We tied her to . . . *look!*" She pointed to a tree, around whose trunk part of the tether was still knotted. "It must've broke."

Charlie was already up. He ran over and picked up

the rope. "It's been *cut!*" he cried, staring. "Someone's gone and cut it!"

The outlaws dropped down from their trees and
came slowly toward them, keeping a wary eye on the
elephant. Charlie held the rope up, showing the cut
end. "Who'd have done that?" he asked, bewildered.

"Jerry!" one of them said immediately, and the
others agreed. "Yeah, bet it was Jerry. Outa spite. 'E
'ad 'is knife all the time, 'idden in 'is sock."

One of them added reproachfully, "You didn't
ought to've said she 'ated 'im. 'Urt 'is feelings. Expect
that's why 'e sloped off."

"Must've made off early," Pete said. "There
weren't no hollow in the bracken to show where 'e'd
slept."

"No," the others agreed. "We looked all over."

"No sign of 'im."

"I ain't worried," Billy muttered. " 'E weren't really one of us. Was 'e, Jo?"

"No. Just tagged along."

Belle got the impression that none of them had
liked him much. When she asked anxiously whether
he would tell the police about Tessie, they all laughed,
seeming to find the idea of Jerry's going anywhere
near the police highly comic. "Not 'im! 'E's on the
run," they said.

Jerry did not go to the police. He rang them from a
phone booth.

"I got something to report," he said in his hoarse

voice. "There's two circus kids 'iding out in the forest. They've stole a helephant."

There was a muffled sound at the other end of the
wire; then a voice said politely, "May I have your
name and address, please, sir."

"They're 'iding up in Foxleap Enclosure—"

"Just a minute, sir. May I have your name and
address first. Then we can both get on to the elephant."

Jerry put the telephone down and swore. Make fun
of him, would they? He left the kiosk and walked
moodily down the high street in the thin sunlight,
pushing rudely past the early shoppers. Suddenly he
stopped and stared in a window. Behind the glass
there were newspaper cuttings fastened to a board,
and several glossy photographs; simpering children in
fancy dress, a beaming man holding up a silver cup,
some men in evening dress, grinning at the camera
. . . Jerry stared at them, hating them all. He looked
up. Above the window was a sign saying: RHIND-
HURST WEEKLY ADVERTISER.

He frowned at the lettering, his lips moving as he
spelled out the words. Then he opened the door and
went in.

" 'Ow much will you give me for a scoop?" he said.

The young reporter did not care for Jerry. Nobody
ever had, that was his trouble. There was something
very off-putting about his large, clumsy figure and the
podgy cheeks encrusted with acne. Though he had
washed the mud from his face, it was not an improve-
ment. Yet, oddly enough, it was the spite in his small,

dark eyes that made the young man take any notice of his story.

"You expect me to believe that?" he asked, half believing it.

"It's true. I can show you where they're 'iding."

"You're seriously telling me that an elephant was kidnapped two days ago and nobody *noticed?*"

"They dunno it's gone, see? The farm people think it's at the slaughter'ouse, and the slaughter'ouse thinks it's at the farm. I told you."

"What's the farmer's name?"

"Dunno. They wouldn't say."

"These circus children, Belle and Charlie, wasn't it you said? What's their surname?"

"Dunno. They didn't say."

"Name of the circus?"

"Dunno. They didn't say."

"They don't seem to have trusted you much, do they?" asked the young man, looking at Jerry with distaste. "What about the parents? Didn't they report the children as missing?"

"They gone off to America."

"Just went off? Without making any arrangements for their children?"

Jerry looked at him blankly, seeing nothing unusual in that. In his world children were often abandoned.

The young reporter hesitated. It seemed a fantastic story—was it even worth checking? Then he looked back at Jerry and decided it was. That heavy, sullen face did not belong to a practical joker. After all, he had nothing much to do till four o'clock. And Foxleap Enclosure was only six miles from Rhindhurst.

Pete and Charlie were on lookout duty. They lay hidden in the tall bracken that edged the graveled walk, talking idly in whispers. Charlie told Pete about life in the circus, about putting up the big top in a high wind with the canvas fighting you and the ropes burning your hands. About hot tea and toast in the dawn, before the hard day's work; about the horses and the elephants, the trumpets and the drums.

Pete told him about the forest. "Funny, ain't it?" he said. "I was brought up in a town. Never thought much of the country before. We came 'ere with the school once. Nature trip. Never saw nothing—too busy assing about with me mates. But living 'ere, it's different, some'ow. It gets you. Seen any deer yet?"

"No."

"We 'ave. They 'ide up in the day. Come out early or when it's getting dark, stepping down the paths like they was wearing 'igh 'eels. Dainty walkers, they are. And we seen badgers, too, and fox cubs playing . . ." He smiled at Charlie, his teeth very white in his dark face. "Think I've gone soft, doncha?"

"No," Charlie said. "I wish I could see them."

"Ain't the right time now. But if you stay, I could show you. Show you where to find marsh gentians and orchids, too. Know what that is?" He held out a small yellow flower.

"No."

"Yellow pimpernel. And that's dog mercury. Betony. Wood spurge. I got their names outa a book. Snitched it from the back of a van," he added, looking sideways at Charlie with a sly grin.

"You ought to be a forester," Charlie said, referring to Pete's learning, rather than the way he'd picked it up.

"Who, me?" Pete said. "Don't make me laugh." But his face was nowhere near laughter. It looked, for a moment, bitterly unhappy.

"Why not?" Charlie asked. "I bet you'd be good at it. Couldn't you—"

Pete interrupted him, saying angrily, as Flick had done, "Oh, you don't know nothing! You're only a kid!" Then, seeing that Charlie was offended, he explained, "They wouldn't 'ave me. I ain't clean. Got a record, see? Most of us 'ave, except Billy. Dunno why. Daft, really." He was silent for a moment, chewing a stalk of grass, his face bleak. "It ain't what we want!" he burst out. "Living in concrete 'utches! Cooped up at school, watching the telly at night . . . we ain't like that! We need . . . oh, I dunno. Something different. We ain't thick, whatever they think. Flick's clever. And I ain't no dumbbell. You know"— he laughed and looked at Charlie—"you know, I bet I could've invented the wheel."

"The *wheel?*"

"Yeh. I know it's been done before. Everything's been done before. The 'ole stinking world's gone stale. It's all been parceled out and there ain't nothing left for us. It ain't even human no more. Pressing buttons . . ."

He saw Charlie staring at him and pushed him playfully, saying, "Don't mind me, kid. Dunno what I'm talking about, do you?"

"Sort of," Charlie said doubtfully.

"You're lucky. You got something."

"What?"

"An elephant," Pete said, and they both laughed.

It was warm and pleasant in the drowsy sunlight. Charlie forgot they were supposed to be lookouts and lay back, gazing up at the sky. But Pete had been well trained. His restless eyes, always moving backward and forward, always checking, saw the distant figures as soon as they came into view.

"Blimey, 'e's fetched the pigs!" he said, and, crouching low, bolted through the bracken into the forest. Charlie followed. Once in the safety of the trees, they ran like hunted foxes, their hearts thundering till they reached the outlaws' lair.

"Flick! Flick! Jerry's fetched the pigs. They'll be 'ere in a minute!"

There was an orderly confusion. The outlaws scurried around like ants, grabbing up their possessions. One of them—Bert, it was—picked up the saddlebags, half empty now, and slung them over his shoulder.

"Follow us," Flick whispered.

They ran through the trees, leaping over fallen logs and arching roots. Tessie, with Belle running beside her, kept up with them easily, crashing through the obstructions as if they did not exist, leaving a trail behind them as wide as a bulldozer's. When they had run for about five minutes, Flick stopped them, and they stood poised, listening. They could hear voices, faintly, in the distance.

"That's them," Flick whispered. His sharp eyes looked around, noting the crushed bracken and trampled bushes behind them; and on one side a wide stream, almost a river, flowing sluggishly between its banks. "Get 'er in there," he ordered. "Pete, you take Jo and lay a false trail. Quick, now! Meet up in shortlands, the dead pine. Okay?"

The youths nodded, splashed their way across to the far bank, and ran off, crushing the bracken and beating down the bushes with sticks as they went. Flick jumped into the stream and, beckoning the others to follow, ran swiftly through the water. Only when the stream narrowed a little, with dense bushes crowding the banks, did he slow down. "Quiet, now," he whispered. "Walk careful. Try not to splash."

It was difficult not to make a noise. There were stones and dead leaves in the mud at the bottom of the stream, and it was very slippery. The children lifted their feet high and slid them into the water like fish, but the elephant, of course, had not understood. She wallowed happily behind them, stopping now and again to suck water noisily up her trunk. Flick frowned angrily over his shoulder, but there was nothing Belle could do.

Now they came to a fallen tree spanning the water.

The outlaws ducked underneath it, leaving the circus children and the elephant on the other side.

"Bleeding 'ell," muttered Flick. He looked at the banks, but they were high and steep here, crowned with matted bushes. "We'll 'ave to—"

"Look out!" Belle cried.

The elephant had lowered her great head and was pushing. The youths raced away, their feet transforming the brown water to flying diamonds. Now the fallen tree was shifting, tearing through the shrubs on either side. Branches cracked like pistol shots, the echoes ricocheting through the forest. Great rocks splashed into the stream. For two yards the elephant drove the fallen tree before her, like a mud guard. Then its top branches met something immovable and it swung sideways, letting her through.

They hurried on, taking no care to be silent now, until they could go no farther. To Charlie's surprise the stream seemed to run straight into a short brick wall, with wire fences on either side. Then he saw it was a bridge, the shallow arch barely clearing the water. On the other side of the fences there was a wide grass verge, a narrow road, and then the forest began again.

"Bill, Dave, lookouts!" Flick said, and the two youths climbed quickly over the fence and ran forward to take up positions at the roadside.

Then Flick turned and stared at the elephant, looking for the first time at a loss.

"What the 'ell we going to do with 'er?" he muttered.

"She can push that fence down easy," Charlie suggested.

"Yeah? Get us all caught, that would! Nothing bugs the foresters worse than broken fences. They'd be swarming all over, trying to find what done the damage. And *they* ain't blind."

He stood frowning while the children watched him. Then he shrugged. " 'Ave to dump you. Sorry," he said regretfully, a general abandoning three of his soldiers for the sake of his army. "Once they got you, they won't look no further. Come on, Bert."

He climbed over the fence. Bert, the saddlecloth still over his shoulder, began to follow.

"That's ours!" Charlie protested, catching hold of it.

"Was yours, y'mean." Bert grinned and jabbed him in the ribs, so hard that Charlie let go and staggered backward.

"Flick!" Belle cried. "Flick, *please!"*

Flick turned. Belle had led the elephant out of the stream and was standing by the fence, looking very small and fragile beside the huge creature.

"Oh, let 'em 'ave it, Bert," he said, perhaps out of true generosity or possibly because Bert, made nervous by Tessie's proximity, had already dropped the saddlecloth and was making off over the grass.

Flick hesitated, looking back at the children with a strange expression, half sad, half envious, as if they possessed something else he knew he could never have. Then he said, "Bye, circus. Been nice meeting you," and was gone.

20

He'd deserted them! Left them out like titbits on a plate, for the police to gobble up while he and his gang made their escape.

"Get her to smash the fence," Charlie said furiously. "I hope they all get caught, rot 'em! Come on, Tessie, stamp on it, trample it down. . . ."

But Belle stopped him. "We'd be the ones caught," she pointed out. "We can't hide as easy as them. Not with Tess."

"What else can we do? We've got to get out somehow."

"I'll do it. I'll get her over. Easy. You be lookout. Go *on*, Charlie!"

Lookout! he thought angrily as he climbed the fence and ran toward the road. She'd have said "keep watch" before. Now it's all lookouts and scouts—Flick and his phony army! Bitterness rose in his

throat, sour as vomit. He'd liked Flick, *admired*
him. . . .

Then he stopped, hearing Belle's voice behind him.
"Hup! Hup! Hup!" she was saying, and he turned
in time to see the elephant rear up on her hind legs, as
she had been trained to do in the ring. But it was
Belle, not Mr. Murphy, who was facing her across the
low fence. And it was bumpy, slippery grass, not sawdust, beneath her feet. Like a tottering mountain she
wobbled, her enormous forelegs like great rocks
poised above Belle's head.

Belle was too near, Charlie thought. She hadn't allowed herself enough room. . . . A muscle in his leg
jumped, as if telling him to run and snatch her out of
danger.

He did not move. Long training kept him from dis-
turbing a performer's concentration. The elephant
took a wavering step forward. . . .

"Down!" Belle shouted, and it was as if a mountain
toppled.

Then the elephant was straddling the fence, her
front legs on one side, her back legs on the other. All
were safely planted in the grass, nowhere near Belle.
She had not even had to jump out of the way.

Charlie let out his breath—and heard, too late, the
sound of a car coming.

"Hide!" he shouted, knowing there was no time.
Belle did her best. Leaping up, she caught hold of a
low branch and pulled it down to form a thin, leafy,
inadequate screen.

Now the car was in plain sight. Through its open windows they could hear the radio warbling:

> "Oo-oo-oo,
> What a pretty bird,
> Oo-oo-oo,
> Is she gonna fly away?
> Oo-oo-oo . . ."

The driver, a young man in a pink shirt, was looking straight ahead, whistling out of tune to the music. It seemed impossible that he should miss seeing Tessie peeping over the leaves, like a large lady hiding behind too small a fan. But he never turned his head. Never slowed down. The car was there, before their eyes; then it had swept down the road, trailing its silly song behind it, "Oo-oo-oo," and it was gone.

"Sorry," Charlie said guiltily. "I didn't hear it in time. I was watching you."

He could not have found a better excuse. Belle preened herself.

"Good, wasn't I?" she said, beaming. "Mr. Murphy couldn't have done no better. Now we've got to get her hind legs over."

The wire was sagging under the elephant's belly, the two posts leaning inward at a drunken angle.

"Come and hold her head a minute," Belle said. "We'll have to chance the cars. Got to take a few risks."

So Charlie held Tessie's head while Belle, tapping each leg in turn, guided the huge feet as they lifted over the dipping wire. "That's it. Anything coming?"

"Can't hear anything."

"Best straighten up a bit."

Quickly they pushed the posts upright and fluffed up the crushed bracken with their hands. It didn't look too bad. Not from a distance.

"Anything coming?" Belle asked again.

Charlie ran down to the road. It was empty. About a hundred yards away he saw a gateway into the forest on the other side.

"Quick! Follow me!" he shouted, and ran toward it, hearing Belle and Tessie behind him.

There was a sign on the gate. At the top, in large letters, it announced: SHORTLANDS ENCLOSURE. Charlie did not stop to read the small print but swung the gate open to let Belle and Tessie through. They found themselves on another wide, graveled path, with the forest pressing in on either side.

"Take her in this way," Charlie said, pointing to a long drift of dead leaves. He had learned something from the outlaws. When Belle and Tessie were tucked among the trees, he raked over the leaves with a stick before following. Flick would have been proud of him. Damn Flick!

They went on and on, deeper into the forest, wishing there were more bushes. Once they stopped dead, hearing voices horribly close.

"Beautiful, isn't it?" an invisible woman said enthusiastically, and another replied, "You should've seen it when the rhododendrons were out. You've missed the best of it."

They crept away, not knowing where they were going, terrified of suddenly finding themselves in a picnic site, or surrounded by tents. The forest grew thicker and danker. The saddlecloth, which they had thrown onto Tessie's back and fastened too loosely in their haste, kept catching in branches and slipping sideways. Now the ground squelched under their feet. Pale, bloated toadstools poked up like blind white eyes. They pushed through a dark-leafed shrub and came upon another stream, shallow and choked with debris, so that the dirty water slopped over the ground on either side. There was a foul, rotting stench, as if something had died nearby and had not been buried.

It seemed a secret, shunned place. A hiding place, for who would come here willingly? Except perhaps the police, beating down the undergrowth methodically, dogs smelling out an all-too-pungent trail. . . .

"How many coppers were there?" Belle asked, and was astonished when Charlie said he had only seen one man with Jerry.

"One?"

"Yes. In plain clothes."

"How did you know he was a policeman?"

"I didn't. Pete said . . ."

They stared at each other and began to laugh helplessly. They wouldn't try to find the outlaws, they decided. They would stay here.

The editor of *The Rhindhurst Weekly Advertiser* looked at his young reporter.

"Mmm—mm," he said.

"What do you think?"

"Oh, it's a great story. I love it. 'Kidnapped Elephant in Yald Forest.' 'We Couldn't Let Poor Jumbo Die, Say Circus Children.' A great story. *But.*"

The young reporter looked anxious. "But . . . ?"

"But I'd be a lot happier if you'd actually seen the elephant. With your own two eyes. Or better still, through a camera lens. A vanishing elephant is a bit much to swallow, sonny."

The young reporter looked crestfallen. He had had a horrible time. His face was scratched, his new jacket torn, his shoes ruined. Stumbling around in the unkempt forest with that lout, he had done everything except see the blasted elephant. He had heard it crashing through the undergrowth—and had fallen flat on his face when he gave chase. He had smelled it —the whole place stank like a zoo. He had been shown droppings as large as footballs, branches torn off trees, carrots and wisps of hay lying on the ground. . . .

Rabbits, foxes, deer, the editor kept suggesting, shrugging his shoulders.

But one thing could not be so easily explained away. In a patch of damp ground by a stream there had been a vast footprint, big as a hubcap.

"I took a tracing," he said eagerly, holding out four pieces of lined paper, on each of which a wavering pencil line described part of a circle. "I couldn't get it all on one page," he explained. "I only had my notebook with me."

"A camera would have been better," muttered the

editor. He spread the four pages out on the desk. "What's this meant to be? Oh, that way around, is it? Still doesn't look like anything," he said. "No, sonny, you need a bit more than this. A few hard facts. *One* would be better than nothing. All this is too airy-fairy."

"I could find out what circuses have gone bankrupt this year," the young man said eagerly.

The editor shook his head.

"Just look up the number of the Thorpes at Goosebeak Farm for me, son," he said.

"Goosebeak Farm?"

"I should have taken on a local lad. Goosebeak Farm, sonny. On the Salisbury Road, some six or seven miles past Bradnam. The Thorpes rented part of it to a circus for their winter quarters. Beecham's—no, Peachem's, that's it. Hadn't heard they were closing down. That's what comes of taking a month's holiday in Portugal. Everyone goes to sleep while I'm away. You should have picked that up. Local Circus Goes Bankrupt. The Big Top's Last Spin. Clowns on the Dole. Good grief, son, you want to smarten yourself up."

The young reporter flushed miserably and removed a frond of bracken from his sleeve.

"Your wits, I meant, not your flipping clothes. . . . Ah, Mrs. Thorpe? Good afternoon. This is Jack Walker of the *Rhindhurst Weekly Advertiser*. What's this I hear about Peachem's going bust? Yes. Yes. They've packed up and gone already? You don't happen to know where I can get hold of two of the chil-

dren. Belle and Charlie . . . Marriot, did you say?
Belle and Charlie Marriot. On a barge? Mmm. Mmm.
If you can just let me have the aunt's address. . . .
And there was one other thing, I heard they had to
have an elephant put down. . . . When was this?
Monday? That would be Barstow's, wouldn't it? No,
I quite understand. Nothing else to be done in the
circumstances. Mmm. Mmm." He listened for some
time, making occasional notes. Murphy, he wrote,
Bradnam General Hospital.

When at last he rang off, he clicked his fingers at
his young reporter.

"Quick. Get me Barstow's of Summaton on the
line," he said.

His call to the slaughterhouse was brief. When he
put down the telephone, he was beaming. "What a
story we've got here, sonny," he said, unblushingly
claiming half of it. "Too good to keep to ourselves.
Now, who will pay best? By the way, where's that
young thug gone? I thought you said he'd be coming
back."

"He said he'd be back at two."

"He's late. Didn't give him any money, did you?"

The young reporter blushed again. "Only a fiver."

"Never mind, sonny. You'll learn." The editor
turned to look at the map pinned to the wall behind
his desk. "Wonder where the devil they are?"

"I know which way they plan to go," the young
man said, and traced a line across the map with his
finger. "The girl showed them, apparently."

"Over Black Ridge, eh? Toward . . . Blanstock

Safari Park! That must be where they're making for. Probably planning to go down on their knees and beg the Duke to save their elephant. What a story! Here, let me arrange a reception committee for them." He started to dial the number of the *Daily Planet* in London. As he waited for them to answer, he looked out of the window. The sky was dark, heavy with rain clouds. "Poor little devils, I hope they look out for the bogs. 'Children Brave Bogs to Save Beloved Pet. Elephant Lost in Black Bottom. . . .' "

21

It was already dark and wet. Wet sky, wet earth, wet woods, wet elephant. They had done what they could for Tessie. At seven, when the rain had started, they had spread one of their ground cloths on her back, where it looked like a pocket handkerchief. So they had given her the other one as well, and, putting up the hoods of their anoraks, crouched miserably under a dripping bush.

It did not help to think of the outlaws, sitting warm and dry in the cinema at Bradnam or shooting down space invaders in the amusement arcade. They had too much sense, Flick had said, to stay out in the rain. When the weather was bad, they went into the towns and only came back to the forest to sleep.

"Don't your hideouts get damp?" Belle had asked, and Flick had laughed, saying, "We don't sleep in them, chick. Too like a grave. We use them as store-rooms. We got tents to sleep in."

"Lucky devils," she said enviously, wiping her wet face with her wet hand. "Perhaps I'll join them, Charlie, after we've settled Tessie."

For they had liked her, she knew. They thought her brave, not knowing she had lost her nerve, and were impressed, not revolted, by her scar. Once Flick had said to her, when Charlie was not around, "Come back in a few years, chick, when you've grown a bit. I think I could fancy you." And what else did she have to look forward to? An unremembered aunt, a new school where she would be bottom of the class, her circus skills unwanted. . . .

"They're *thieves,* Belle," Charlie said.

She and Charlie had been brought up strictly, even if Mrs. Marriot's morals were practical, rather than high-minded. "What d'you think you're doing, girl?" she'd asked once when she'd found Belle going through her handbag. "You want to watch it! You're an artiste, remember, not a thieving gypsy. Traveling circuses *travel.* Abroad, sometimes. How'll you get a permit if you got a prison record as long as my arm? Eh?" It had been no good, Belle saying she was just looking for a hanky. She'd had her bottom slapped.

Then, a year later, something had impressed her more than her mother's hard hand. On a wet, muddy Sunday it was discovered that a tent boy had gone off with the week's takings. She would never forget the desolation, the cold wind blowing, the guv'nor's wife in tears. . . . And then the whole circus had gathered around, patting the weeping woman on her shoulder and holding out a hat into which they had put their hard-earned money. How proud she had felt to be one of them, an artiste, a worker, putting her fifty pence in with the rest.

The circus was over now, and her career all smashed up. But at least they had known it once, the belonging, and could hope for it again. She thought of Flick, saying, "What have they ever done for me?" Meaning—nothing. Only the forest was kind to him. But then she remembered Billy coughing, pressing his thin hands to his chest, and Flick's anxious look. She remembered their faces when she had asked tactlessly about winter. Perhaps, cold and wet as they now were, she and Charlie were still the lucky ones.

"I ain't going to be no dropout," she said. "I'm going right to the middle where it's warm."

"What are you on about?"

"Dunno. I was thinking of the big top. All the trailers with their windows lit up. And rabbit stew."

"Oh, shut up!"

At ten o'clock they could bear the leaking forest no longer and decided to move. Because they did not know exactly where they were, they came out of the trees a good mile from the track Belle's finger had traced on the map, and did not see the waiting cars. They crossed the road silently and unobserved.

The rain had dwindled now. In the distance somber clouds swept down to the humped back of Black Ridge, so that it looked a mere reflection of other hills in the sky, as if the world were upside down. The heath itself was blurred, its contours disguised by a misty drizzle so that bushes might have been elephants or elephants bushes, for all one could tell.

"Nobody'll see us in this muck," Charlie said. "I can hardly see myself."

Belle looked back. The road was already invisible, but on the left a few hazy lights shone dimly through the mist. One of the forest villages, perhaps. Or a farm. She turned her back on the thought of a warm kitchen and looked at the gloomy wilderness ahead.

"Which way?"

"Dunno. Straight ahead, I suppose."

"Got your compass?"

"Too dark to see it, and we'd best not show a light yet. Let's go on."

At first they led Tessie. The ground was rough and bumpy, bisected with narrow streams and bristling with small bushes, seen too late. The elephant seemed unhappy at their slow, halting pace and rumbled mournfully, pulling against Belle's restraining hand on her ear. Belle worried about her, frightened that she would catch cold.

"If we rode her, she could go faster and keep warm," Charlie suggested.

Belle was silent.

"We'll never get there if we don't. It's a long way."

She hunched her shoulders and walked on without answering.

"You won't fall off again. I'll hold on to you. Just pretend she's a double-decker bus. . . ."

"I ain't afraid!" Belle said furiously.

"Then why don't we ride her?" he asked, sweetly reasonable.

She scowled at him. He gave a reassuring smile. Both expressions were wasted: their faces were dim blurs in the dark. After a weary pause Charlie switched on his torch, shielding the beam with his fingers, which blossomed like red flowers in the night.

"What are you doing?"

"Looking at the compass," he said. "Which way do we want?"

"Left on the map."

"West," he translated.

"And a bit down."

"West sou'west?"

"Dunno," she said sulkily, not caring. "Sounds all right."

They stumbled on in silence for a while, then Belle gave in.

"All right. You win. We'll ride."

"Not if you don't want to," Charlie said airily. She could have hit him and said so. For a moment, wet, hungry, and exhausted, they hated each other. For two pins they'd have walked off in different directions . . . except that it was too dark and desolate to be alone. So they mounted Tessie and rode on in silence.

The elephant walked fearlessly over the dim heath, taking bushes and streams in her stride. Belle, sitting in front and clinging to the headband, was soon too tired to be frightened. She peered through the wet darkness until the blurred hills seemed to be swaying before her eyes. She was rocking, rocking in a boat. Waves slapped against the sides . . . She jerked awake, clutching the headband to stop herself from slipping off.

The rain had stopped now, and a watery moon hung in the cloudy sky. The elephant was walking strangely, unevenly, dragging her feet. And still Belle could hear a sucking, splashing sound. . . .

"It's a bog!" she screamed. "Charlie, Tessie's gone into a bog!"

His arms jerked around her waist. "Wha-what's the matter?" he mumbled.

"Stop! Tessie, stop!"

The elephant stood patiently. Charlie switched on his flashlight and shone it down. At first the ground looked firm enough, covered with low, small-leafed bushes and round hassocks of grass. Then they saw the gleam of dark water everywhere. On the left tall reeds grew thickly.

"What shall we do?"

"Turn her around. Go back."

But Tessie, for the first time, was obstinate. She did not want to go back and ignored Belle's shouted orders. When Belle kicked her leg against the leathery neck, the elephant sucked up a trunkful of muddy water and tossed it over her shoulder, soaking the children.

"What's the matter with her?"

"Dunno."

"Perhaps there's a deep hole behind her."

"Can't be. She got here all right."

"Why won't she turn around, then?"

"Perhaps she can't. Perhaps she's sinking!"

Terrified, with some idea of lightening the poor animal's weight, they slid off her back, landing in the soft, sodden bog myrtle and, stumbling to their feet, only ankle deep in thin mud. The elephant started to walk forward again.

"Stop!" screamed Belle. The elephant stopped and sighed.

"Perhaps we ought to trust her," Charlie said. "Flick said the bogs weren't very deep."

They looked at each other helplessly, not knowing what to do. They shone their flashlight around in a circle, but there was no telling where the bog began or ended. It all looked much the same, dark and dreary, stretching away into the mist. It might be safer to go on. The elephant's heavy weight might have disturbed the unstable ground behind them, setting it quaking like a black jelly.

"It doesn't seem very deep here," Charlie said, prodding the wet ground with his foot. "I'll walk in front. Then, if I start sinking, Tessie can pull me up and we'll try another way."

"No, Charlie! I don't want you to!"

"We can't stay here."

So Charlie walked ahead, shining his flashlight on the ground, stepping from hassock to hassock and testing the depths in between with his foot. Once he slipped and went up to the knee in thick water, feeling the mud beneath clutch his ankle. He could not help crying out, but before Belle and Tessie could reach

him, he was safe again on a bush, only lacking one
shoe.

"Don't bring her this way," he shouted. "There's a
sort of hole. Take her around by those bushes."

"Charlie, let's go back! It ain't safe."

"It's not too bad. It's only deep in patches."

"Let me go first, then."

"No."

"I want to!"

"You're better with Tessie. She wouldn't obey me."

This was true, so Belle gave in, though she dreaded
seeing Charlie vanish before her eyes, leaving only a
few bubbles breaking in the mud. She was crying
now, keeping so close behind Charlie that he kept
shouting at her to keep back. She did not even notice
the ground getting firmer beneath her feet until Charlie suddenly gave a whoop of triumph and started
capering around, waving his flashlight like a mad fire-
fly.

"We've done it! We've done it!" he shouted. "It's
solid!" He stamped on the ground. "Well, almost."

It was the only bog they came across. Now the
ground began to rise steeply, and there were sharp
stones between the bushes. They walked for a few
miles, to give Tessie a rest. It helped to keep them
warm. There was a cold wind blowing, and their
clothes were wet. But Charlie had put on his
gumboots, and his feet were soon sore, so they rode
again. Up and up they went, two children and an
elephant, crossing the Black Ridge against the night
sky and vanishing out of sight.

22

It was a cool, moist morning, still damp from the night's rain. At six o'clock the two children, carrying a sponge bag, towels, a large scrubbing brush, and a bucket, let the elephant out of a barn and crossed a field to reach the stream on the other side.

"We'll have to do it early," Charlie said. "There's just nowhere to hide. Not unless we go back into the hills."

"And we ain't doing that. Flipping map! Green for woodlands, it says. Ten trees and six bungalows, call that woodlands? This water ain't all that clean, Charlie."

"Cleaner than us."

"It's cold. I ain't stripping."

"Just wash where it shows."

Having done their faces and hands, they set to work on the elephant, dousing her with buckets of water and scrubbing everything they could reach. Back in the barn they changed into clean, though creased, clothes, tucking their denim trousers neatly into their gumboots. They combed their hair carefully and smoothed it down with their hands. Belle, glancing apologetically at Charlie, rubbed the damp soap over her scar and stuck a strand of hair over it.

"Got to look respectable," she said. "How's that, Charlie?"

"You'll do."

But somehow there was still a touch of the circus about them, a vagabond air. Perhaps it was the swagger in their walk, the slight exaggeration of their gestures. Or it might have been the rim of dirt around their shining faces.

"Do you think it will work?" Belle asked.

Charlie shrugged, then, seeing her face, said, "Of course it will!"

"It must. I couldn't bear it if . . . It *will* work," she said, defying fate.

She gave Charlie a cheerful grin that cracked his heart. He did not think her plan stood a chance. Even if they got Tessie in, sooner or later the safari park would count their elephants, find they had one too many, and chuck her right out again. But he could not tell Belle this.

"Dunno why I'm so nervous," she said uneasily. "I wish . . . I wish I wasn't such a coward."

It was the first time she had ever admitted being afraid. He said quickly, "You're not! You're very brave. You've just lost your head for heights, that's

all. It's nothing to do with being brave. It's sort of like
being ill. You can be cured."

But Belle was thinking of a dragonfly she had seen
in the forest, glittering and dancing over the stream
with an easy, careless joy. Belonging in the air. "I'll
never be a high-flyer no more," she said. "Still,
who cares? Not me. Only, I do want us to save Tessie. . . ."

"We *will*," Charlie said, feeling he'd kill anyone
who stopped them.

At seven they came out from behind a high hedge,
about a quarter of a mile from Blanstock Safari Park,
and began walking up the side of the road. They
seemed angry and upset. Holding sticks in their
hands, they drove the elephant in front of them, as if
they were frightened of her. Every time she turned
her head to look at them, they leapt back nervously
and said, "Shoo! Go away! Shoo!"

A few minutes later they had an audience. A farm
truck came rattling around the corner, swerved
wildly, narrowly missing the ditch on the other side,
and stopped.

Charlie ran forward, shouting, "An elephant's gotten loose from the safari park! We're trying to drive
her back!"

The driver stared at him, at Belle, at the elephant.
"You're those—" he began.

Belle interrupted him. "It frightened Star—"

"That's her pony," Charlie said.

"I got thrown off! I'm bruised all over."

"She might've been killed."

"We're going to complain."

"They should keep their elephants off the road."

Under this barrage of indignation the driver appeared bemused. He kept looking at the elephant, opening his mouth, shutting it again, and looking back at the elephant, as if he did not know the best thing to do. Only when Tessie, bored, began ambling toward the truck did he make up his mind. He released the handbrake.

"You're going straight to Blanstock, then?" he asked, eyeing the approaching elephant uneasily.

"Yes. It ain't safe to leave her straying," they said virtuously. *"You* nearly had an accident."

"I'll let them know you're coming," the driver said. "Keep her away from my truck, there's a good couple of kids. It's new." And he drove off.

"Quick!" Belle said, and they began to hurry.

Timing, as Mr. Schneider had so often told them, was the essence of a successful act. They wanted the gatekeeper flustered, half asleep, only too glad to fling open the gates and get the elephant off the road before the park could be accused of negligence. They didn't want to give him time to think. They didn't want him to use his telephone.

They raced down the road, only slowing when they reached the corner. Now, at last, they saw the great gateway to Blanstock Safari Park before them. The farm truck was parked on the verge just past it, and there were other cars beyond. The driver was standing and talking excitedly to a small group of men, and they all turned to look at the children as they herded the elephant down the last stretch of road.

The gates were opening! They'd done it! They were going to get Tessie in! It was all Belle could do to stop herself from leaping around with joy and triumph as Tessie walked slowly and with enormous dignity through the tall wrought-iron gates.

Then the world seemed to explode. Bright lights flashed in Belle's face. People crowded around her and Charlie. Men with cameras . . . *policemen . . . !*

"No!" she shouted. "No!"

Pushing through them, she ran over to where the elephant was standing patiently and flung her arms around Tessie's trunk.

"No! No!" she wept. "Oh, Tessie, we did our best."

And she felt Charlie's arm around her shoulder and, turning, saw that he was crying, too.

23

It was this photograph that was to dog them for the rest of their lives; pinned to the bulletin board of their new school, turning up years later in old magazines, lining the drawer of a boardinghouse in Bognor, and found, framed and flyspecked, on the wall of a café in Brighton. There they were, caught forever, crying like babies. There even seemed, by some trick of the light, to be a tear shining in Tessie's round, solemn eye.

The effect had been tremendous. Everyone wanted Tessie. The story of the two children, kidnapping their favorite elephant to save it from the slaughterhouse, had gone to the hearts of the public, just as the editor of *The Rhindhurst Weekly Advertiser* had thought it would. People sent money. A Save Tessie Fund was started. Three circuses, suddenly warmhearted, offered to take her. And so did the Duke of Blanstock. Unlike the many small children who wrote to offer homes for Tessie in garden sheds or spare bedrooms, *he* had a safari park.

So, with Mr. Murphy's blessing, that was where Tessie stayed.

"She's old, like me," Mr. Murphy said. "She deserves a rest. And the duke's a gent. He won't turn her out when the public has forgotten her."

He never had his cottage at the gate. Though out of the hospital now, he still needed to be looked after. So he went to live with his sister in her council flat in Worthing, where he kept, strictly against the rules, a pet snake.

"You should call it Tessinose," Belle said, eyeing its questing, grayish length.

Mr. Murphy smiled and shook his head.

"Christabel," he said, "that's what she's called."

Belle blushed at the compliment, even though she was not overfond of snakes.

They could hardly believe their luck. Instead of being punished they were everyone's darlings. They felt very warm toward the world . . . even though they knew, in their heart of hearts, that had Tessie rioted, smashed property and people, they would have been not darlings, but thoughtless little monsters. The difference had been the whereabouts of Tessie's feet.

Thanks to Tessie's gentleness and good sense, they were heroes. In public they behaved with becoming modesty. But it was too much to expect the same in private. In Aunt May's respectable sitting room they gave way to sudden fits of shrieking laughter and wild cartwheels. Smilingly Aunt May removed her more delicate ornaments.

She was no longer the thin, cool gray lady of their memory. She had put on weight and a pink blouse and had become fat and jolly. Best of all, she obviously liked them.

A telephone call was made to Belle's parents in America. Aunt May had tracked them down to a small town in the Midwest. Their voices, squeezed through thousands of miles of wires, came out as small and excited as the children's. Aunt May smiled ruefully. Circus people never really grew up, she thought. It was only when her feckless sister and brother-in-law proposed that Belle and Charlie should take instant advantage of their temporary fame and come to America that she put her foot down.

"School," she said, taking the phone firmly from Belle. "They've got to go to school, Annie. That's what we agreed."

Belle's parents reluctantly gave in, comforting themselves with the thought that children who had begun by kidnapping an elephant would be sure to go on to even bigger things.

So they went to school. It was on the first day, walking through the windy streets, that Charlie noticed Belle's hand go up to her face in the old nervous gesture. She had not done this for weeks. Not since the forest.

"It hardly shows," he said.

"No."

They walked on in silence. They came to the school: it looked like a prison. On the pavement outside there was a crowd of chattering children. On Belle and Charlie's approach they stopped and stared. Uneasily Belle reached for Charlie's hand.

"We've done it all before," he said. "In a week we'll be old pros."

"Yes."

Charlie made a noise like a roll of drums. "Positively the First Appearance before any Public! The Sensational Christabel and Cosmo! Remember?"

Belle smiled and nodded.

Now they had reached the other children.

"Hello," said Charlie boldly. "We're new."

"Hey, aren't you those circus kids?" a boy asked, inspecting them carefully. "The ones in the papers?"

"That's us," Belle said. She was stiff with fright. It made her look arrogant.

The watching faces turned hostile.

Then a gust of wind blew down the street, sending old bus tickets dancing down the pavement and whipping aside Belle's carefully arranged hair. All eyes went to her scar. Charlie clenched his fists.

"Oh, snot! And I spent hours fixing it," Belle said crossly, pulling at her hair. "Old Scarface, that's me!" She made a rueful clown's face and laughed.

At once the hostility vanished. Who could resist a clown? Belle, the practiced performer, had won over her audience. She had them in the palm of her hand, thought Charlie. Admiringly he watched as she disappeared in a crowd of girls, all eager for the privilege of her friendship.

They liked the school, maybe because the school liked them. Belle worked hard, having gotten it into her head that she'd like to be a zoologist. Or a vet.

"I'm good with animals," she said, with her old incurable boastfulness. "The duke says I'm amazing."

Charlie was disconcerted.

"Aren't you going back into the circus?" he asked.

"Dunno."

"Belle, you *must*! Mr. Schneider said we could both have a job at Christmas. Not only me. You, too."

"Big of him." She tilted her nose and said grandly, "The duke said I could come and help at the safari park on vacations. They like me there. The keepers say I'm a wonder."

"Oh, Belle!" he said, laughing.

"It's true."

"You've *got* to stay in the circus. Or I won't marry you when I grow up," he said, looking at her slyly.

And she tossed her head, smiling, and said, just as she had done so long ago, "You'll be lucky."

In the late autumn sunlight two masked figures are dancing on the grass, like sequined dragonflies. The clown, it appears, is in love with the ballerina. He blows her kisses, walks upside down, and somersaults in front of her. She does not seem to see him but dances as if in a dream, serious and self-absorbed.

Now the clown holds up his hand, and a yellow

rose blossoms from his fingers. He offers it to the ballerina, who takes it. Then she dances on. Round and
round she goes, faster and faster, to sink at last into a
deep curtsy. The clown bows.

There is a round of applause, and people shower
coins into the clown's hat. "It's them. It's Belle and
Charlie," they tell one another. Then they get back
into their cars and drive off to see the baboons and the
lions and, of course, the elephants. Especially their
old favorite, Tessie of Yald Forest.

Blanstock Safari Park is doing well. The admis-
sions have trebled since they took in the circus elephant. Everyone loves her. The duke likes the children, too, who amuse him. They are staying in
Blanstock for their half-term vacation and coming in
to help with the animals. Belle has a natural gift with
them, and he hopes to persuade her to take a job at
Blanstock when she leaves school. Charlie, he under-
stands, is to be a circus star. Sitting on the grass,
wrapped up in their new winter coats, for it is cold in
spite of the sun, Belle and Charlie are counting up
their money.

"Not bad," Charlie says. "Eighty pence more than
yesterday."

They have started a new fund. They are saving up
to buy a safari park, with a small circus on the
grounds. They know it is only a dream, but they like
dreaming.

"After all, the duke's got a fairground here, so why
not a circus?" Charlie says.

"We'll just have clowns and acrobats and high flyers," Belle suggests. She has become uneasy about performing animals.

"And Star Spinners?"

"Yes," she agrees, smiling. "We'll get a couple of kids and train 'em."

They are happy. They hardly ever think of the outlaws. Only sometimes on a cold night, when Belle hears the rain beating on her windows, she wonders about Flick and Pete and Billy and what will happen to them when winter comes.

About the Author

Vivien Alcock, a commercial artist, lives in London with her family. *Travelers by Night* is her fourth novel. Her first three, *The Haunting of Cassie Palmer; The Stonewalkers* (a *School Library Journal* Best Book), and *The Sylvia Game* were also published by Delacorte Press.